THE REMAINING

A NOVELIZATION BY
TRAVIS THRASHER

TYNDALE HOUSE PUBLISHERS, INC.
CAROL STREAM, ILLINOIS

Visit Tyndale online at www.tyndale.com.

Visit Travis Thrasher's website at www.travisthrasher.com.

TYNDALE and Tyndale's quill logo are registered trademarks of Tyndale House Publishers, Inc.

The Remaining

Designed by Dean H. Renninger

The Remaining is a work of fiction. Where real people, events, establishments, organizations, or locales appear, they are used fictitiously. All other elements of the novel are drawn from the author's imagination.

Library of Congress Cataloging-in-Publication Data

Library of Congress Cataloging
Thrasher, Travis, author.
The remaining : a novelization / by Travis Thrasher.
pages cm
Summary: "Just after a young couple says their vows, the earth shakes, and some people die suddenly and are taken away. The rest of their wedding party and friends are left to wrestle with what happened and with their faith"— Provided by publisher.
ISBN 978-1-4143-9752-8 (sc)
I. Remaining (Motion picture) II. Title.
PZ7.T411Rem 2014
[Fic]—dc23 2014024633

Printed in the United States of America

20 19 18 17 16 15 14
7 6 5 4 3 2 1

THEN THE SEVEN ANGELS WITH THE SEVEN TRUMPETS PREPARED TO BLOW THEIR MIGHTY BLASTS.

REVELATION 8:6

(NEW LIVING TRANSLATION)

PROLOGUE
FOREBODING

1

The visions predicting the end of the world began during a week spent on the beach in Wilmington, North Carolina, a week that was supposed to celebrate love and life and tomorrow.

There. I actually admitted it on paper. Or at least on a computer screen.

My name is Lauren Hall. I'm a twenty-seven-year-old black woman who grew up in Wilmington. The only reason I'm writing this now is that I don't know who to talk to. I love my friends, and I'm scared for them—for all of us—because of these visions.

The visions. It sounds like something you might hear

about in an old Southern church with the snake charmer and the blind woman in the wheelchair suddenly walking *and* seeing. I've gone to church my whole life, but I'm not blind, nor do I need a wheelchair.

Lately, however, I've felt like I might need a shrink. And no matter how many times I've prayed and how many times I've waited on God's Word, I keep seeing strange things.

I no longer question whether something's going to happen.

My only question is when.

2

There was only one objective for the trip to NC: for Dan to propose to Skylar. Well, let's make that two objectives. The proposal, and the total and complete secrecy surrounding it.

It's amazing how something as simple as meeting at a college party could ultimately result in something as complex and intricately planned as that last week in July. Skylar, of course, had no clue, and even some of the rest of us didn't know all the details. Dan had chosen to tell only those who could be the most tight-lipped. So that meant that out of the gang, Tommy knew almost nothing, Jack knew about as much, Allison knew a few more tiny details, and I knew the most. Dan knew me well enough to know I could keep a secret or two.

We'd had this trip planned for some time, so it wasn't like Skylar was suspecting anything. The woman who loved to plan everything in her life (and I mean *everything*) surely wanted to have some kind of say in the ring she'd be wearing and the date she'd be getting married. No, I take that back. I think Skylar really wanted to propose to Dan. And she wasn't ready to, not just yet. So Dan beat her and surprised her.

He surprised all of us that week, actually. It really was a remarkable buildup to an amazing moment.

If only I hadn't been so completely terrified by then of what was to come.

3

It started the night before I was supposed to leave for Wilmington.

I'd gone out with Blake to dinner and then to see a movie. It wasn't like we went to see some movie about demons or ghosts or something like that, though I've never been bothered by horror films and I can't really recall the last true nightmare I'd had before that night. I couldn't blame it on the dinner, either. It was an enjoyable date night with the love of my life, the man I'd be spending a week away from.

I finished packing when I got home and went to bed just before midnight. Nothing unusual.

I woke up that night around three in the morning. Sweaty, breathless, worried, even guilt-ridden. I knew I had to say a quick prayer just to get my heart and soul back in order.

I'd seen things that didn't make sense, that still don't

make sense even now. Skylar in a bloody wedding dress. Dan running, his face full of tears, his anguish obvious. I wanted to help them but I couldn't. It was like I was watching them on display through a window on the street. I could touch the window and even bang on it but there was nothing I could do to break through the glass and help. Not one thing.

And that was only the beginning. When I turned my back, I could see the flames from burning buildings and the rubble from explosions. People screaming and crying—the ones who weren't lying dead in the middle of the street or on the sidewalks.

I started to run (isn't that what people do in dreams?) but I couldn't go anywhere to escape the carnage. Each turn led me to someone else I knew who was hurting. Allison. Jack. Even Tommy.

It was just a dream, of course. I knew it was. My mind turning this time with all my friends into something terrible. I was thinking about them and the upcoming proposal and the future wedding.

But the images of all the people I loved most hurting and crying and bleeding were unsettling. And simply bizarre. I didn't know where they were coming from.

It took a while to fall back asleep that night.

The next morning I simply dismissed the nightmares as just that and nothing more. Nothing worth telling anybody about. Just a mental glitch due to a busy schedule and an overactive imagination.

Yet something inside, some persistent voice, told me it was something else.

I ignored this voice. At least for the time being.

4

Our group came together during our college years. Thinking of them now is similar to thinking about family members you've grown up with and love. When a face comes to mind and makes you smile. That's how I feel about this group. I love these people.

Dan Wilson is the all-American guy. Our young Harrison Ford. Tall, dark, and handsome with a bright future. He was a smart guy long before meeting Skylar at a party and knowing she was the one, but the fact that he realized this and pursued her only made him seem that much wiser.

Jack Turner was Dan's childhood buddy growing up in Wilmington. As kids they were friends simply because they were both involved in sports and had a lot of similarities. While Dan's the all-American, Jack's more of the heartthrob. He's the Tom Cruise of the bunch, the good-looking athletic type who always seemed to be surrounded by friends.

I met these two because of my friendship with Allison Costa. She was a classmate I got to know the first two years I was at Duke. If it hadn't been for my mother and her ailing health, I wouldn't have transferred to UNC Wilmington before my junior year. But I know that was something that God chose to allow for a reason.

And sometimes his reasons remain unknown to us.

Allie and I continued to be close friends even while I was gone. I relied on my girl a lot during those years when my mother fought her cancer and even after she passed. It's amazing how God puts just the right people in your life at the exact time you need them. Allie kept me sane while my faith kept me hopeful.

What can I say about Allie? She's good people. She's got a good soul. She's an honest, outspoken, and sometimes even fiery Italian. I've always loved her because I never need to wonder where I stand with her. It's no wonder Jack fell for her. They've been dating for over six years now. I've wondered just how serious it is, but Allie doesn't really like to talk about it. And now it's Dan beating Jack to the punch, proposing to Skylar before Jack can make it official with Allie.

Skylar—"the girl next door," a cliché I hate using but one that really does fit her. I'll be honest since I'm writing this to myself and nobody else. I didn't like Sky when Allie first introduced us. I felt like I'd been replaced. Here's this beautiful blonde who's vivacious and well-to-do with wonderful parents and a wonderful life and surely a wonderful dog, too. Or so I naturally thought. And the selfish person inside of me went, *So I'm losing my friend to this chick while I'm dealing with my mother's cancer? Thank you, LIFE.*

But while Skylar might *look* like the girl next door, she's got an immense heart. I know that now.

At my mother's funeral, one thing stood out more than anything else. It was something Skylar did for me. So simple yet so meaningful. She showed up at the funeral and came over to give me this huge hug. She'd come to the wake the night before and had been one of the many people I barely remembered seeing. But that morning, as I stood filled with an ocean of grief I didn't know what to do with, Skylar gave me a tiny little bag.

"These are violet petals," she said to me.

And that was it. She hugged me and let me be.

My mother's name was Violet. So during the funeral, I remember clinging to that bag of petals as if somehow squeezing them might bring my mother back. Or at least take away the pain of losing her.

I still haven't told Skylar how much those petals meant to me. Or how much that simple gesture still means to me now.

5

Snowprints on the sand in the summer. I could see them stretching out for miles.

The snow fell in huge flakes, and normally I might dance around with an open mouth, but now I ran in terror. Running to find someone to tell. Running to try to figure out what exactly was happening.

Again, I knew I was dreaming. Sort of. My feet felt lighter. The touch on the ground felt softer. Yes, it was snow on sand, such a strange mix. But I knew it wasn't real.

Yet the terror wrapped around my heart felt authentic. It was pure. Even if I knew it was unnecessary.

I hadn't been this afraid since first learning about my mother's cancer. And then it took months and months of desperately giving it to God before I learned to let it go.

This feels like something impossible to let go.

I ran to find someone to tell. Not to help me but to help them.

If you knew the world was about to end, what would you say? Or maybe the question should really be, if this world was going to end, whom would you tell?

I could see the sea, ripe and red. The color of blood. The color of death.

I ran and glanced back at bloody tracks I was making.

I was bleeding myself, though I didn't know how and couldn't figure out why.

And this was when I woke up. Still out of breath. My feet felt wet.

I had been at the beach house only one night, but already the dreams were seeping into my mind, heart, and soul.

I could only hope the tide would eventually take them all away.

6

I was grabbing coffee that first morning at the beach house when I saw Tommy coming up to me, carrying that video recorder of his.

"Listen, Scorsese," I told him, "it's a little early for filming, isn't it?"

"Never."

Tommy Covington was the lovable comic in our group, the guy who seemed to love life the most and always seemed to be at odds with it too. He was the moodiest one out of the three guys but also the one I knew the best.

"Everybody else still sleeping?" I asked.

"Late night last night," he said, a question in his voice. I hadn't joined them.

"I needed some sleep," I told him.

"Oh, come on. You've gone soft on me already."

Tommy ended up being nice and set his video camera aside. I knew he'd be shooting a lot this week, leading up to the big moment.

If Tommy Covington could do anything in the world, it would be to direct motion pictures for Hollywood. But I don't see Tommy doing that. Oh, I'd never tell him to his face. I could see him maybe doing a small indie flick or two. But he doesn't seem to have the Hollywood kind of persistence.

Then again, I might be wrong about him.

I remember the first time I met him, when he came up to me after seeing me at a party I'd attended at Duke University. I was going to UNC Wilmington by then but still liked to go to parties with Allie at Duke on the weekends. Tommy was at UNC Wilmington too, and we ended up realizing the connection we had with our friends. There was definitely a connection between Tommy and me too, at the beginning. But Tommy was never someone I could imagine myself being with long-term. The fact that my mother probably wouldn't have been thrilled about me bringing home a white guy had nothing to do with it; it just wasn't meant to be. And eventually someone else would capture his attention.

"Looks like we're going to have great weather," Tommy told me.

"I can't wait to sit on the beach and put on my headphones and veg out."

"Oh, no. Come on—I have activities for us to do."

"Activities? Like what?"

"We're going on a cruise. Beach volleyball. Bicycling into town. Beach football."

"Oh, and let me guess," I said, joking. "Beach . . . soccer?"

"No vegging out this week." Tommy paused. "Think Sky knows anything?"

"No. She's too much of a control freak to imagine Dan would plan all this to propose here."

"Hope she doesn't get mad."

I only shook my head.

"What?" Tommy asked.

"Skylar won't be upset."

"How do you know?"

"I saw the ring."

7

That makes Skylar sound so superficial. She can be, but so can anybody else. And what girl doesn't dream of the perfect guy and the perfect house with the white picket fence? Okay, maybe my perfect house doesn't have a fence around it but rather happens to be fenced in by the woods, but regardless. Skylar's a girl. And Dan wasn't going to upset her.

The nightly ritual turned out to be sitting on the beach around a campfire. Everybody would be tired and giddy and full and warm from the day's sun on their skin. We would laugh and tell college and post-college stories. We imagined how our lives would be in one year or five years or ten years.

Even there, in the midst of so much happiness, I felt prompted to finally say something about my dreams and the worry I was carrying around with me. Tommy even asked me in front of everybody what was wrong.

For a second, I almost told them. *Almost.*

"I'm fine. I'm just tired."

"Oh, come on, Lauren," Tommy said. "You were just crying with laughter, and then all of a sudden we start talking about the future and you become a zombie."

"How are things with Blake and you?" Skylar asked.

"They're good. Really."

"So are you guys pretty serious?" Allie asked.

"Yeah."

"Something's wrong," Tommy said.

"Nothing's wrong."

"Why so glum, then?"

I only shook my head. I wanted to tell Tommy to leave

me alone and stop prying. I wasn't about to tell them my dreams. Not as a group. Not in this setting.

Nothing ruined the mood like telling everybody I was seeing visions of their deaths and the end of the world.

I might—*might*—tell Allie at some point. And the only reason I'd do that is to have her convince me I wasn't totally losing my mind.

"Maybe Lauren has something else to tell us," Tommy said, still pushing.

"Wait a minute," Jack said. "Lauren, are you going to be a mommy?"

Leave it to Jack to go *there*.

"You know my thoughts on that. You know it would take a miracle for that to happen."

They all knew where I stood when it came to purity and waiting for marriage. And I definitely didn't want that subject to be talked about on this night.

Jack was a little extra animated from the generous amount of beer he'd had. Nothing unusual, just Jack being Jack.

Thankfully, discussion moved away from me and onto other things.

Thankfully, nobody ended up asking me about my mood again.

8

I could see them all out on the boat laughing and dancing and having the time of their lives. I was on the shore, watching and waving and listening. I called out to them, but they were too far away.

It was nighttime, and I couldn't understand why they hadn't told me about the boat outing. Maybe I'd gone to bed early, but shouldn't they have told me they were planning to head out onto the water later? Now the music and laughter and waves were all too loud for them to hear me.

The boat began to head farther and farther out to sea. And then something happened.

Flames rose from the boat.

I could now hear the sound of screams. They couldn't simply jump off. They were trapped. Burning.

And as the boat and my friends became glowing ashes floating in the middle of the night, my heavy breathing and my pulsing heart and my sweaty forehead soon told me this was just another nightmare. I was in bed. My friends were fine.

For now.

9

"You okay, Laur?"

I'd held it together and kept my craziness from everyone. But Allie eventually caught me at a quiet moment in the house while the rest of the crew was out on the beach.

"Yeah, I'm fine," I told her.

"It seems like something's going on."

"I'm just tired."

"That's what you said yesterday," Allie said. "Seriously—what's going on?"

By now I'd made a promise to myself: don't tell anybody until *after* the wedding. Nobody needed to know I saw the wedding party dead on the floor before the groom had even proposed to the bride.

"Laur?"

"Tell me something," I said, not deciding to tell her but simply taking another route. "What would you do if you knew tomorrow didn't exist? If this was the last day of your life?"

"Sounds like a soap opera," Allie replied with a giggle.

"Serious."

Allie came and sat by me, then put an arm around me and gave me a half squeeze. "That's what this is about," she said.

"What?"

"This. The last outing. The final hurrah. Then one by one, we're going to go our own ways. Some together, but not *all* together, not like this."

I smiled. "Yeah, I guess that's it."

"We'll always be friends," Allie said.

"How do you know that? A bit idealistic, isn't it?"

"I think friendships or any relationships take work. And I know you, Laur. I know how hardworking you are. You're tenacious. Kinda like Skylar but in a different way. Sky's tenacity is in getting her own way. Yours is in making sure others do."

Now she was genuinely starting to make me tear up. "That's one of the nicest things I've ever heard."

"Well, I've been around the boys, so I haven't had a lot of nice things to say."

We both burst out laughing.

"I'm going to miss this," I told her.

"What? This place? The beach? *Me?*"

"You, of course. Always. But no—this place in life. I keep looking ahead and all I see are responsibilities and burdens and weights. Some good. But all weighing me down."

"You'll always have me to come lighten your load," Allie said.

I forced a carefree smile. Something told me I wouldn't.

Something told me Allison wasn't going to be around much longer.

And this feeling baffled me, and even made me feel a bit guilty inside for thinking such a crazy thought.

10

Each day during the week, Dan did something special for Skylar. Nothing over the top that would cause her to think something was happening. He was always being sweet to her, so this wasn't anything new. But each thing somehow involved the rest of us. One evening we went through snapshots of the last half decade when all of us knew each other. Another was an evening out with just us girls (paid for by Dan). Another centered around watching Skylar's favorite movie, *My Best Friend's Wedding* (complete with matching dinner and sing-along from the scene we all knew).

Little by little, Dan was giving Skylar gifts. And they were smaller and smaller items until the last, which would be a tiny box with a ring inside.

But really, it wasn't gifts Dan was giving to Skylar. He was ultimately giving her—and the rest of us—something we'd never let go of.

Memories.

That final night, we were all tired and giddy and both ready to go back home to normal lives and sad to leave this place behind. We did the nightly routine around the fire pit on the beach.

And that was when Dan finally paved the way to asking the big question. We didn't know how he was going to do it, but we did know we would be there.

"Okay—I have a game I want us all to play," Dan said. "I want to know one question you're burning to ask. The number one question."

"Questions we're wanting to ask each other?" Jack asked.

"No—just questions you have."

"About what?"

Dan shook his head at his friend. "About anything. Life in general. You can ask anything to anybody."

"What if you don't have any questions?" Jack asked.

We laughed and mocked him and he was amused with our response.

"What? I'm being honest."

"Jack Turner," Tommy said, joking. "The ultimate blank slate."

"Come on," Dan said. "It's confession time. Jack just needs a few minutes to wake his brain cells up."

"Ha-ha."

Skylar went first. No surprise there.

"I've always wanted to ask my parents something. I've always wanted them to tell me if they're just faking it. If they really, truly are that in love with one another."

"That's awful," Tommy said.

"What? I'm being honest."

"Your parents are crazy for each other."

"I know, I know," Skylar said. "It's just—I wish I knew their secret. Or if they're just really good fakers."

We laughed and couldn't believe she actually thought that. Everybody knew the Chapmans. They weren't faking it. Granted, I'm sure they had their struggles, though it was hard to imagine.

Each question seemed to get a little deeper and more personal.

I brought up the whole having-kids thing with Blake. It was a subject that we hadn't talked about yet, simply because I didn't want to be the girl who asked the question about how many kids he'd like. Blake didn't seem too interested in kids in general and never, ever, *ever* said something like, "Man, I can't wait to have a couple of boys or girls one day." He never went there. So of course I was genuinely curious.

"So just ask," Tommy eventually said.

"I don't want to even go there. I mean—we're barely talking about the future and all that. I don't want him feeling pressured."

Tommy's question revolved around his father and what he *really* thought of Tommy's current career and life direction. It was an obvious choice for Tommy, since he spoke often about his clashes with his parents.

When Jack finally got serious, he opened up about his hope and desire to play some kind of professional sport and the door that had closed since college. I knew it had been tough for him but didn't realize *how* tough.

For all of us, the vulnerability being expressed was special and rare.

These were all such great people.

Allie finally began to speak. But as she started to talk, something happened.

It's like she was going to say something and then changed her mind.

"I guess my question—my questions—are just general ones," she said. "Ones I have that anybody could answer. I would just like to know if all these things I want to do—things I hope to do in the future—will ever come true. Will ever actually happen. Sometimes it seems like I have too many lofty goals and plans, and then I think I'm not even anywhere close to doing all of those. It's overwhelming."

"You can do it," Skylar said. "How's *that* for an answer?"

Allison laughed. But something told me she had wanted to share more. About what, I didn't know.

We talked more about the future and things we wanted to do and things we hoped would happen. This lasted for about twenty minutes and even I forgot that Dan hadn't said anything.

"Wait a minute," Skylar said, breaking the conversation. "Dan—you didn't even give us your big question."

"Oh, that's okay. I enjoyed all of yours."

The fire crackled in front of us and the stars glowed like tiny little embers in the night. Dan had an arm around Skylar and looked comfortable and even almost tired.

Little did I know Mr. Dan Wilson could be such a good actor.

"Oh, come on," Skylar continued. "You have to have some question. Something about the job?"

Dan acted like he was considering. This was when I began to think, *Wait a minute, he might actually propose to her.*

"I guess the biggest question I have is like lots of yours. Where I'll be. I mean, I wonder if I'll be able to do this night after night, week after week, year after year."

"Do what?" Skylar asked.

"Be next to you."

That's when I think all of us knew, including Skylar. Her eyes grew wider as she turned to get a good look at him. Suddenly she noticed Dan wasn't tired and he wasn't neglecting his question and he wasn't only moderately interested.

"Dan?"

"I want to know if the girl I've spent the last few years dreaming about and loving would still like me around day after day. Will she grow tired of me? Will I be able to make her happy? Will she still laugh at my jokes? Will I be able to always be her knight in shining armor? These questions and ten thousand other ones all revolve around this girl I'm madly in love with."

We were all smiling and silent while Skylar turned to face him.

"Dan . . ." she said in a soft voice.

"No. Here's the thing. There's really only one question I want to ask. One important question that can change my whole life. But it's one you have to answer. And I wanted to ask it to you in front of our closest friends. I wanted to surprise—"

"Yes!" Skylar said, wrapping herself around Dan before he could get any more words out of his mouth. "Yes, yes, yes."

They embraced and kissed and we all clapped and laughed.

"Let him finish," Allie said.

"Isn't there supposed to be a ring?" Jack asked.

"I wish I had my camera," Tommy said.

"I wish this night could last forever," I ended up saying.

And I was being truthful. I wish the night didn't have to end.

Dan finally managed to say the words to Skylar and show her the ring. She definitely wasn't saying no now. No way. Uh-uh.

We sat around the campfire for a long time. None of us wanted to go to bed. We wanted to take this one last chance to be together and be young and not worry about tomorrow.

Little did any of them know I *was* worrying about tomorrow. I was worried it wasn't going to arrive.

I felt like I still had so many things I wanted and needed to say. But for the rest of the night, I remained silent.

The silence still haunts me.

The world hasn't ended. My friends aren't dead. The wedding is right around the corner. Everything is fine, right? So why do I still feel terrified? Why do I still get the feeling something is coming that none of us will be able to escape from? What is God trying to tell me?

I wish I knew.

1
CAMERAMAN

Everything goes black.

For a minute, Tommy can only stand there freaking out. His heart races.

Not now. Not today. This is so not happening.

But as quickly as the screen went blank, the camcorder bolts right back to life, just as a high-definition video recorder should do. Especially one bought just this year for over twelve hundred bucks. Of course, it's not one of those professional cameras that cost close to five thousand. Tommy Covington might be good, but he's not *that* good. Or that successful. Not to own one of those machines.

Maybe not yet.

He's on a sidewalk right next to the river, facing the hotel, doing the kind of work a second unit on a film crew might do. Capturing some shots on location for mood and for setting purposes. No actors, no lines to be said. It's just background work, the stuff usually done by a team Tommy hopes to one day be a part of.

Before I become the next big-name Hollywood director like Christopher Nolan.

Seeing the world in the rectangular frame of a camera's viewfinder puts things into perspective. For the past half hour, Tommy has noticed things about the city of Wilmington he's never really seen before. Having grown up in the Chicago area, he still feels more like a Midwest guy than a Southerner. Yet he has no intentions of moving back north. All of his family are still living in the Chicago suburbs, but his *true* family is here in this city. Many of them are here in this hotel.

Two of them are actually getting married today.

Tommy aims the camcorder at the hotel. The Plantation is one of those luxury places that Tommy wouldn't be able to afford now or even probably five years from now. He's already captured the fancy logo and impressive entrance in a digital file. Later on, when he begins to assemble the video, he'll do some fun things with this footage. Perhaps some narration, definitely some cool music.

Dan asked him to do this as a favor, knowing that he'd do a good job. "Make sure Skylar likes it," was all Dan had to say. Skylar, Tommy knows, has this way of bringing out the best in people. Granted, they might be angry and in tears by the end, but everybody wants to please Skylar. Especially the man marrying her.

So far, Tommy has gotten a number of important pieces of the city on film. The Cape Fear Memorial Bridge. Riverfront, the intimate seafood restaurant where Dan took Skylar on their first date. The small balcony where they ate. The coffee shop they often frequented, a place Tommy spends way too much time at. The pub all of them liked to go to on weekends, a place Tommy spends way too much money at. All pieces of the puzzle that represent Dan and Skylar. Soon to be Mr. and Mrs. Wilson.

Tommy thinks about the past month and realizes it's been quite possibly the best month of his life. Maybe because he's been around the gang so much, enjoying the final month of summer. Maybe because of what Allison, the maid of honor, said last night in an emotional toast at the rehearsal dinner, that this wedding was really going to change everything.

Maybe she's right. Maybe this will *change everything.*

Tommy has gotten hours of footage on video since Dan proposed to Skylar at the end of the summer a year ago. The beach house they all rented, the proposal that all of them helped with. Tommy can only hope that his own engagement and wedding—if that ever happens—will be half as memorable as Dan and Skylar's. But then again, it's Dan and Skylar. They should have their own trademark and brand. Maybe a reality television show.

And I'll be filming it.

Of course, before Tommy proposes and gets married, he probably needs to start dating. That's probably a necessity.

His phone buzzes, and he checks out the incoming text.

It's Allison.

I'm so not going to make it through this day.

Tommy smiles at the text and sends a quick one back.

You'll do fine. And who knows? Maybe someone else will propose today.

The text is simply supposed to be an encouragement to Allison. He pauses for a second on the sidewalk, waiting for a response. But none comes.

Very typical. He's used to waiting.

Sometimes it seems his whole life revolves around watching and waiting. Watching for the right moment, waiting for the right memory to capture.

Hoping for that perfect minute where everything finally comes together.

He's a patient man. He doesn't mind watching and waiting.

Tommy heads into the hotel, ready to capture some more moments on film. He has a feeling this day will indeed change everything

Tommy opens the hotel room door and finds Jack standing there half-dressed, listening to his iPod and not stressed about anything. Typical Jack Turner, already running late and acting like the world revolves around his schedule.

"You gonna put the rest of your suit on?" Tommy asks but doesn't get a response.

He moves over to Jack and pulls one of the earbuds out. Then he steadies the camera to get some more footage.

"Jack, you have anything to say to Dan? This is it, man. He's the first one of us to get put on permanent lockdown."

The smile appears, the one that has always made girls like Allison and all those others go gaga over Jackie-boy. Mr. Football Star, not quite talented enough to be the next Tom Brady but certainly handsome enough to play the part.

Jack steps a little closer. He's a bit taller than Tommy, a bit more broad-shouldered. A bit more everything, in fact. "You know, if you're gonna shoot the wedding, you should probably be wearing some pants."

With the quickness of a star quarterback, Jack grabs the already-loose pants on Tommy's rented suit and pulls them down to his knees. Then he moves directly in front of the camera lens. "Dan, today is your day, my friend. We are happy to be here to share it with you. Tommy even wore his lucky boxers." He reaches out and forces the camera onto Tommy and his favorite boxers, the ones with bacon all over them and the phrase *Bacon makes everything better* written in various places.

Tommy pulls his pants up and then backs away to redirect the camera off his boxers. He aims it back at Jack.

"We love you, brotha!" Jack screams.

"Don't mock the bacon boxers," Tommy says with pretend seriousness.

"Never. Only respect."

"That's right. Now, you gonna come upstairs?"

Jack shrugs. "We still have an hour."

"Where's our main man?"

"He's all tuxed out. Stopped by a few minutes ago for a beer."

The fridge in Jack's hotel room is probably as full as the bar up on the rooftop.

"Did you charge him?" Tommy jokes, turning off the camcorder and buckling his pants back up. "You almost broke the button, you moron."

"It's nice to see you in a suit, looking all responsible. You should try it out more often and burn those concert tees."

"You already sound so corporate. When'd you turn so old?"

"One of us has to," Jack says as Tommy leaves the room.

Tommy finds the comment ironic. Out of all of them, Jack is the one who seems least likely to grow up. He doesn't mind playing the game of being a manager at a financial company—a position his father helped him get—but he still isn't about to suddenly "grow up." Whatever that term even means.

"I'm going to find our groom before he decides to call everything off," Tommy says over his shoulder.

Jack only laughs, knowing Dan wouldn't call anything

off. Knowing that if Skylar suddenly decided to do something like that and run away, Dan would follow her. He would do anything for his lady.

It's a nice thought. Doing anything for your lady.

One day maybe I'll be able to do anything for someone.

One day maybe.

But today is not that day.

Dan Wilson's perfectly styled hair is the first thing Tommy sees when he enters the men's room directly off the rooftop hallway. Tommy is already recording and aims the camera at the soon-to-be groom.

"How you feeling, buddy?"

Dan's head pops up, and his surprised look soon turns to annoyed amusement. "This better not make it into my wedding video. You can stop shooting while I'm in the bathroom."

The groom looks tall, dark, and handsome in his black tuxedo. Tommy isn't about to ruin this glorious moment by shutting off the camera. "I left my car running outside just in case you want to bolt," he jokes.

Tommy pans the camcorder to the mirror behind a set of sinks. Dan enters the picture and stands next to him. As always, Dan looks calm and collected. Tommy would be sweating by now if his own wedding ceremony were only an hour away.

"Your car's a hunk of junk," Dan says. "We wouldn't make it out of the parking lot."

"We can hijack the limo, then."

"You know what you need? You need to find a good girl like Skylar," Dan tells him, washing his hands.

Tommy moves his head away from the viewfinder and looks into the camera in the mirror. "Groom wisdom. Nice."

"There's nothing better than being in an honest, committed relationship. I think—"

"Seems a little hard to take relationship advice from the dude who just joined a church because his fiancée wouldn't marry him otherwise."

Dan smiles. "The girl gets what she wants."

Both men hear the sound of a toilet flushing. The door to one of the stalls opens, and the handsome older man stepping out greets them with a confident smile. "Gentlemen," Skylar's father says with quite a bit of irony in his voice.

Mr. Chapman makes Tommy feel a bit nervous anyway, and now this.

Tommy and Dan both greet the bride's father as he starts to wash his hands. Dan gives his groomsman one of his look-what-you-did-now glares, then uses Tommy's suit as a towel for his wet hands.

Tommy shouts out a *hey* but gets promptly ignored by the groom, who heads out of the bathroom.

For a second Tommy contemplates interviewing Mr.

Chapman, then gives him a courteous smile before following Dan. He figures he's got enough bathroom footage for one day. He still has to interview the rest of the bridal party and get their candid thoughts before the big event begins.

It still blows him away that he's here—that they're all here. His best friend is getting married. And so it goes. Life happens and you can't help it.

You just hang on for the ride.

It's going to be a memorable day. Tommy plans on enjoying every single moment.

2
THE BRIDESMAID

"Isn't it the bride or the groom who usually end up having second thoughts about the wedding?"

Lauren Hall rolls her eyes and wants to throw her cell phone across the room. But that would require too much effort. Right now she's frozen and can't move. Blake's on the other end trying to talk some sense into her.

Lord knows I need a little sense right about now.

"Lauren, we were just talking about this last night."

"And now we're talking about it today."

"Do you want to be late?" Blake asks.

She doesn't need to hear the obvious. Yes, sure, she might be late, but what she *really* wants is not to go. This thing has been building up for a year now, and even though the strange nightmares and visions seemed to go away, lately they've been back. With a vengeance.

"Sweetie, you're going to be fine. You're just anxious about your friend getting married and about letting her down—"

"I'm afraid of thinking I'm losing my mind," Lauren says.

She holds up a perfectly manicured hand that got done earlier this week. She and Allie went with Skylar for a fancy day of getting all spoiled. It was part of Skylar's gift to them for standing up in her wedding.

"Skylar's going to lose her mind if you don't show up."

Lauren knows that's true. Yet she still doesn't want to get up off this bed. She doesn't want to go downstairs. She doesn't want to pick up her dress and then have to go through everything that will follow.

I don't want to let anybody down. Especially Skylar.

"Lauren, remember what I told you?" Blake asks.

Such an assured and confident voice. She loves him so much.

"You told me a lot."

"Let's say the world *does* end."

"Oh, that," she says. "That wasn't very helpful."

"I'm being honest."

"Don't be honest."

"Let's say the world ends tomorrow. What can you do about it? Huh? Tell me."

She shakes her head and stands up. Well, it's a start.

"Nothing," she says.

"Absolutely. Nothing. You can't live in fear of tomorrow. You have to celebrate today."

"Who said that?"

"I'm saying it. What? You think it's a quote?"

"I'm sure it's a quote."

"All right then, I'm quoting someone. Mr. Anonymous."

"Okay, okay, I'm heading out of the apartment."

"Well, that's good. I was afraid I was going to have to come and carry you out."

She grabs her purse and keys. "Well, I'd prefer that. Can you still do that?"

Soon Lauren is in her car and driving.

"Look, I need to go too," Blake says. "I'll see you shortly, okay?"

"Thanks for talking me off the ledge."

"There's no ledge here. Only natural anxiety."

"The end of the world is not 'natural anxiety.'"

Blake's laugh is like his voice. Calming. "Just make sure you save me some champagne before everything blows up."

"Not funny," she tells him before hanging up.

She knows Blake is only trying to cheer her up, but it's definitely not amusing. She wonders if she made a mistake telling him about the nightmares. They finally began to stop days after coming back from the trip to the beach last summer. Soon they were long gone, and she felt comfortable enough to tell him about them. He didn't have any sort of big explanation or even much to say at all related to it. He just told her she didn't have to be so guarded about things like that. Not with her friends and especially not with him.

A week ago, the nightmares began again. For no apparent reason. They're the same as they were before. Images of her friends all trapped and dying and suffering. That's the part that bothers her most. Hearing and seeing her friends hurting and suffering is painful.

The drive to downtown Wilmington takes longer than usual. There's a lot more traffic than there used to be when she lived here. She's staying with her father, who lives outside the city. Skylar offered her a room at the hotel but Lauren said this would be a nice opportunity to get some time with her father. She still sometimes feels guilt for not living closer ever since moving away a few years ago.

She turns the radio up to shut out her thoughts. It's a good thing she looks at her phone because she didn't hear the incoming text message.

Are you almost here?

It's Allie. Again. She keeps pestering her.

Lauren speaks her message back into the phone, a slightly safer way to text while driving. But she's stuck on the bridge anyway. It looks like they must be doing some construction up ahead.

Almost there. Traffic.

Hurry up! Allie writes back.

For the moment, Lauren's car is stopped on the Cape Fear Bridge. She looks up and realizes this bridge is a lot like her father. It's always been around. She's so accustomed to using it and passing over it and seeing it in the background. It's a fixture in her life.

Just like her dad.

It took her mother passing for Lauren to finally wake up and realize how important her parents were. It's like being forced to stop and examine the bridge. She had to slow down and stop in order to realize this very important thing was right in front of her.

She closes her eyes and reminds herself she needs to get her dress from the bridal shop before arriving at the hotel.

When she opens her eyes, the sky above her has darkened. It's an angry shade of purple. There are things flying down from the heavens—dark, hideous things.

What is happening this can't be happening I can't be seeing this.

The flying specters are swarming straight down toward her. Lauren holds her breath and covers her face and expects to feel some kind of violent impact.

A car horn makes her open her eyes.

The lane in front of her is empty. The sky is blue again. The bridge intact.

Nothing is flying toward her from above.

She moves her car forward even as she feels the pounding in her chest.

This is ridiculous.

Maybe Allie can give her one of her Xanax pills. That and a glass of wine would do nicely right about now.

God, what is going on? Are these visions from You? Why are You showing me these things?

She gets all the way to the bridal shop before her heart stops racing. She's only minutes away from the hotel. Lauren knows she has to get her act together. Now.

She's got a dress to put on and a friend to support. Her meltdown is just going to have to wait until another day.

3
IT'S TIME

Allison Costa can see the Cape Fear River from her hotel window. Looking out over the rooftops of Wilmington, she sees the familiar sight of the bridge in the distance. The image seems inviting to Allison right now. How appropriate would it be if she got in her car right now and drove over a river with *fear* in its name? Crossing the bridge toward an unknown future far away from this North Carolina city, far away from all the frustration here?

Allison turns away from the striking view and notices another one. The dark-haired beauty facing her in the mirror across the room is quite a strange sight. She doesn't really like getting dressed up, and she especially doesn't like being a maid of honor. But for her best friend, it's the least she can do. She'll gladly wear these high heels and this violet strapless dress. Some brides might fear a dress like this on someone like Allison would overshadow them. But Skylar has no fears.

And there's no overshadowing Skylar Chapman.

Allison looks at the time and knows she needs to get up to the rooftop pavilion to help out with last-minute details. She's the maid of honor, but she's already failed miserably with her responsibilities. The bride is the one who's supposed to be on an emotional roller-coaster ride, right? The bride is the one who's supposed to get all weepy and sappy in front of people when saying thanks and telling them one of the many good-byes? But last night, it was Allison, not Skylar, who fell apart.

As she touches up her makeup one last time, she still feels embarrassed. She can still hear herself babbling on, becoming emotional about losing a best friend, then getting choked up talking about this day they all knew would happen eventually.

This day . . .

A text comes to her cell phone. For a second she thinks it must be Lauren telling her she's finally arrived, but it turns out it's Jack.

Did you decide to bail on us?

That's not funny, she texts back.

After your speech last night, I'm not sure.

Shut up. I just had too much wine, Allison writes.

Yeah, right. Easy excuse. You coming?

I'll be there in a minute.

Tommy's on the loose, Jack says. **Be on the lookout.**

I always am.

She slips the phone in her purse and glances back outside for a moment. She takes a deep breath and lets it out.

It's going to be fine. I'm going to be fine and I'll make it through today and tomorrow we'll see what happens.

That river and that bridge aren't going anywhere. Allison, on the other hand, just might be.

She has to see what happens today. She has to see about a lot of things.

Allison finds Skylar's door ajar and slips in to try and find the bride. Skylar's suite on the twentieth floor has a large living room and kitchen area right next to the bedroom. The front rooms are empty and messy, with clothes on the couch and the backs of chairs. A buffet of appetizers sits out in the kitchen, but most of the plates look untouched. The table in the kitchen has a variety of makeup and hair products on it.

"You look fabulous," Skylar calls out when she enters from the bedroom.

The bride still has her hair pinned up, and she hasn't put her dress on yet. She wears a short silk robe over a pair of sweatpants.

Allison hugs her friend and gives her a big smile. "How are you feeling?"

"Anxious. There are a hundred things that need to be done. Have you seen Lauren?"

Allison shakes her head. "Not yet. I texted her earlier. She was picking up her dress this morning. It needed an alteration after she tried it on last."

"That girl—always waiting till the last minute."

Skylar's makeup looks extra glamorous today. "Good job," Allison tells her, circling a finger around her face.

"My mother helped. You know what a perfectionist she can be."

Allison knows because Skylar takes after her mother. Even in the designer sweatpants, Skylar looks like a Miss America contestant.

"Have you seen any of the boys?" the bride asks.

"No." For a second Allison hesitates to share what she's thinking, but she knows she has to. She has to get it out in the open before the rest of the day happens and the moment is gone. "Sky—I'm sorry about last night."

The puzzled look on Skylar's face tells her she doesn't understand. "What do you mean?"

"What I said. My mini breakdown."

"Oh, girlfriend." Skylar gives her a hug but avoids messing up their makeup. "So far, *that's* been the highlight of this weekend."

"Great. Seeing me totally get all mushy."

"I thought it was sweet."

Allison moans. "I just—I feel so stupid. Jack was laughing at me all night."

"*Jack* is the last person who should make you feel bad about what you said. Seriously."

"I know; it's just . . ."

Skylar comes over and takes her by the hands. "Listen to me. I'm not going anywhere. You're going to be seeing plenty of us. We're not planning on moving out of the city or state, you know. So, what about you? Do you have some bit of news you need to tell me?"

Allison can feel the emotions coming on again.

Stay away tears get away from my perfectly done eyes don't even think about it.

"Well, you know," Allison says, "I do have a secret to tell you."

"Oh, really?"

"Yes. I'm pregnant, and Jack and I are eloping. To Vegas."

Skylar laughs. "Yes. The place you elope to when you're pregnant."

"I'm going to become a card dealer in a casino. Seems like a great place to raise a child."

They both howl out in laughter.

"Maybe that's why you have this glow about you," Skylar says. "You're expecting."

Allison grunts. "At this rate, I'll be lucky to be pregnant by the time I turn forty-five."

A call comes in on Skylar's phone and she takes it.

"Can you help me?" the bride asks her maid of honor after the brief conversation. "They need us in the reception hall. Some last-minute arrangements."

"That's why I'm here, right? To help and support. Not vice versa."

Skylar puts an arm around her. "We're here for each other and always will be. Understand that?"

"Yeah."

Before leaving the room to head upstairs to the roof, Allison pauses for a moment.

"What is it?" Skylar asks.

"Thanks for being you."

"Oh, stop."

"No, I'm serious. Dan is a lucky man."

Skylar's face lights up as bright as her blonde hair. "You got that right. Remind him about that again when you see him."

"I don't have to remind him. He knows, Sky. Trust me. He knows."

"It's good to know *some* men get it."

They share a knowing look, then both smile before leaving the room.

Perhaps this day and this ceremony and this whole thing will help a certain other unknowing man finally get a clue. That's all Allison is going to hope and pray for today. For someone to finally, finally get a clue.

4
PERFECT

Tommy knocks again on the door and waits to see if a bride opens it. He's pretty sure this is Skylar's room, but nobody seems to be inside. He checks his phone for any messages, then starts to walk down the hallway, ready to head back upstairs. A figure rushing toward him makes him laugh. He makes sure to capture her with the video camera.

Lauren Hall's bright eyes look extra animated under her newly short bangs. The light-skinned black woman stops right in front of the camera, the bridesmaid dress in a plastic bag draped over her shoulder. "Seen Skylar?" she asks.

"That's who I'm looking for."

"She gotta be freaking out that I'm late." Lauren

shakes her head and sounds out of breath. She begins to move past him.

"Hold on. I need to get some prewedding advice for the lucky couple."

Lauren doesn't even think before staring right at the camera, her face angling perfectly like someone accustomed to being filmed. "Put the other person's needs first," she says. "You'll be amazed at how strong your love will grow."

Tommy knows she's speaking from experience. He's met Lauren's man, Blake, a big guy who's as crazy about her as she is about him.

As Lauren heads toward her hotel room, Tommy sighs and stops filming. "Maybe that's why I'm still single."

Lauren doesn't even look back as she finds her room key in her pocket. "Quit chasing after the wrong girls, buddy."

"What am I gonna do? All the good ones are taken."

After getting the door opened, Lauren just gives him a sparkly smile. "If I don't put this dress on, someone else is gonna have to take my place. Skylar's definitely freaking out about now."

"I'll find her," Tommy says. "I'll take care of it."

"You're a good guy," Lauren shouts out. "Even if no girl knows it."

She laughs and disappears into the room. Tommy knows Lauren is one of his biggest fans, and she's often joked that she might've tried to bring him home years ago in college if her very traditional mother didn't mind her bringing home a white boy. That's been a constant source of amusement between them, and for years Tommy has joked about the reasons her mother would love him.

He heads back upstairs, assuming he'll find Skylar busy with something.

In so many ways, it seems unlikely that Tommy should be here at the Plantation, pressing the button of the elevator and heading up to find the bride and the rest of the wedding party. This band of friends started when Tommy ended up rooming with Dan at UNC Wilmington his sophomore year of college after attending a junior college the year before. Dan could've gone to University of North Carolina or Duke but chose to attend UNC Wilmington because his father had gone there. Their pairing in a dorm room seemed like a fluke, with Dan being the jock and playing both soccer and basketball. Tommy was the party guy interested in making movies but having no clue what else he wanted to do in his life.

It was through Dan that Tommy got to know Jack Turner. Dan and Jack were friends from the same neighborhood and grew up going to the same schools. They would go up to Duke for parties on the weekends. It was only a couple of hours away, and the parties there were a lot better than those on their campus. Jack was already pretty serious with a Duke girl named Allison, and her best friend happened to be this gorgeous blonde named Skylar. She was attending the rival school on Tobacco Road, UNC, but fate and chance met up at a party at Jack's apartment one night when Dan and Skylar met.

The circle was complete when Tommy recognized Lauren in a class of his and realized he'd had a conversation with her at one of the parties at Duke. She was a longtime friend of Allison and Skylar.

And just like that, the six of them were suddenly inseparable. Another thing Tommy and Lauren joked about was the fact that they weren't a couple while the others were. Sometimes they would pretend like they were one. All in good fun.

If I hadn't decided to go to a junior college my first year, I would've gotten a different roommate at UNC Wilmington. That would've changed everything.

He steps out of the elevator knowing he's a lucky man.

Life's all about luck. All about being in a random place at a random time.

Sometimes your timing just happens to be very good. He thinks about this as he glances around and finally sees Skylar. Then he sees the maid of honor.

Then again, sometimes your timing is just a bit off.

The rooftop of the Plantation is made up of two halves: one half is a large indoor reception room, and the other half is the outdoor deck, where the wedding ceremony will be held.

Moving away from the elevator, Tommy thinks the hallway resembles a beehive that's been turned over. Servers are going in and out of the reception hall while early guests slowly meander around trying not to appear too nosy.

The bride is in the banquet room, just as Tommy suspected. She still doesn't have the wedding dress on, but otherwise she looks perfect with her hair all set and her face made-up like a movie star's.

As Tommy approaches, he can hear Skylar rattling off instructions to the workers. No wonder they're rushing around like crazy people. This is what Skylar does. She makes you crazy. She says jump and you don't just ask how high. You look for a trampoline.

From the entrance to the room, Tommy films Skylar acting like a catering supervisor.

"Captured on film," he says into the built-in microphone, "the elusive Bridezilla in her natural habitat."

He moves closer to her as she stands near a table set for ten. She's working on a napkin.

"Two folds, then one," Skylar says.

Tommy starts laughing and has to fight to hold the camera steady as he films her talking to the servers.

"If this is the most compelling content you're getting, then we may be in trouble."

"I got some great stuff with Dan earlier. You're gonna love it."

"I'm sure," she exaggerates. "I can't wait."

He moves the camera over the table, getting the ornate flower arrangement in the center. "I'm just trying to document your big day. The good, the bad, and the ugly."

"There will be no ugly," she says, staring at the flower arrangement.

A voice behind them calls out in mock astonishment. "Did you just say the word *ugly* at Skylar's wedding?"

He turns and sets the camera's sights on Allison, who moves from table to table helping to straighten out the place settings.

"Here's the maid of honor, ready to assist the bride with whatever Skylar needs. Ready to break down in tears at any given moment."

"Be nice," Allison says to him, not looking his way. "You could help out a little too, you know?"

"I am. I've got you in focus."

Allison turns those dark Italian eyes and lashes his way, then blows a kiss to the camera. Lauren isn't the only one comfortable with being in front of a video recorder. This girl he's facing could be an actress. In fact, she might be acting a bit even right now.

He really wants to tell her how stunning she looks, how the bright bluish purple dress complements her, or maybe how it really does fit her like a glove, but that would be too much. She'd roll her eyes and laugh at his comments. So instead he goes for an easy jab.

"You going to catch the bouquet?"

The playful, busy, and assured air suddenly vanishes. Allison gives him an honest look for a moment, the same expression she wore last night during the toast. Then she feigns being annoyed with him as she quickly brushes past and heads toward Skylar.

Allison stands next to the bride and puts her arm

around her. It's a quick and spontaneous moment, the kind Allison has all the time. Tommy is glad to capture it on film. He likes seeing these two ladies together.

Allison isn't the only one who's going to miss the way things are right now.

With footage of all the wedding party now complete, Tommy decides to get some footage outside on the deck before he gives the camera over to Skylar's cousin Johnnie. Tommy won't be holding the camera during the service. He volunteered but the bride thought it was a bit too much.

He takes in the view of the city of Wilmington. The September sky is blue and perfect for an outdoor wedding. The day is warm but not too stuffy. He can see the bridge and the river from here.

For a second Tommy lets the camera just settle slowly over the city.

"This is pretty great, Skylar," he says. "Your wedding is going to be perfect."

5

AS LONG AS WE BOTH SHALL LIVE

The ceremony moves in sweet slow motion, and Allison takes every moment in with a joyful and jealous spirit. The wind seems to hold its breath as the wedding party walks out onto the rooftop deck and begins marching down the aisle. Skylar's niece, a three-year-old named Charlotte, sprinkles flower petals from a basket as she confidently strides past beaming faces. Tommy and Lauren walk next, arm in arm. Then Jack guides Allison to the altar.

Feeling his arm locked with hers as they approach the wedding arch made of white flowers, Allison tries not to turn the focus inward. It's too easy, and it's too selfish as well. She's here for Skylar and Dan. She's celebrating their big moment with them. One day they'll do the same for her.

Why don't you say for Jack and you?

She glances at her handsome man, and he gives her a bright smile. Jack has always made her feel comfortable and confident, even when those nagging doubts begin to come.

Allison stands next to Lauren; then they all await Skylar. Allison knows what the reaction will be. It will be the same as her own reaction. She was taken aback a bit seeing her friend so glamorous and so beautiful and most of all so happy. You can't paint joy as bright and brilliant as the look on Skylar's face right this instant.

The bride strolls with her father down the aisle, and for a second, Allison peeks over at Dan. He has tears in his eyes as he smiles.

The future so bright, so endless. Like the sky above them.

Music plays and Allison is genuinely happy. The voices that ask when it'll be *her* time and why can't this be *her* moment have all been shoved far back inside and silenced. For now.

Skylar reaches them and for a second she gives Allison a knowing here-we-go grin. It's as if she's floating, and every single face in the crowd is watching her fly away.

Pastor Roberts greets the couple and then everybody else in an amiable tone. He looks younger than his fortysomething age, and he smiles as he recounts his first encounter with Skylar.

"You were about this tall and going into fifth grade when I met you," Pastor Roberts tells Skylar. "I remember saying to my wife back then—this girl is going to break a lot of hearts. Thankfully for Dan, you only made his grow."

The pastor speaks in a natural manner, relaxed and fun. Just like the ceremony. Skylar had said she didn't want some of the traditional elements that her parents wanted. Like the lighting of the unity candle. Like having some kind of singer doing a number during the service. Skylar wanted it quick and easy, and that's how it goes. Soon the pastor is asking them to make their vows.

"Do you, Dan, take Skylar to be your lawfully wedded wife, and do you promise before God and these witnesses to love her, to comfort her, honor and keep her in sickness and in health; and, forsaking all others, keep thee only unto her so long as you both shall live? Do you so promise?"

"I do," Dan says with a big smile on his face.

Allison glances over at Jack, but she can't tell if he's looking at the bride or her.

"And do you, Skylar, take Dan to be your lawfully wedded husband, and do you promise before God and these witnesses to love him, to comfort him, honor and keep him in sickness and in health; and, forsaking all others, keep thee only unto him so long as you both shall live? Do you so promise?"

Skylar gives out a choked and emotional "I do."

Once again Allison can't help looking at Jack.

Don't you ever want this?

The bride and the groom move to face each other, but Allison just keeps watching Jack.

Don't you want to be with me for as long as we both will live?

"I give you this ring as a sign of my promise to you," Dan says. "And with all that I am, and all that I have, I honor you."

He slips the ring on Skylar's finger.

"I give you this ring as a sign of my promise to you, and with all that I am, and all that I have, I honor you."

Skylar does the same.

All I am and all I have and all I've ever wanted . . .

There are tears in Skylar's eyes, just like the ones in Allison's.

Pastor Roberts raises his hands.

"Now, by the power vested in me as a minister of the gospel, I now pronounce you husband and wife. And whatever God hath joined together, let not the hand of man put asunder. We now ask the blessing of the Lord on Dan and Skylar and their life together as husband and wife."

At the pastor's prompting, Dan leans over and gently kisses Skylar. It's a tender kiss, sweet to watch. The crowd applauds and cheers as the couple faces them.

Allison wonders how long the two of them will stay together, and if they'll make it, and if this really will be as happily-ever-after as it appears. She wants to hope and believe they'll make it, that they'll defy the odds and stay together.

Love can prevail. Love can endure.

She wipes more tears away and catches Jack looking at her, smiling, shaking his head at her tears.

You could make a few of these tears go away, buddy.

The newly married couple walk down the aisle. The heavens seem to watch with a grin of their own.

This day really is perfect. Nothing can change that. Absolutely nothing.

6
THE GREATEST DAY OF OUR LIVES

A hundred songs go through Tommy's head as he focuses his camera on the lucky couple. The vows have been spoken and the kiss has been given and the celebration has started. Now it's that in-between time where greetings and hugs and slaps on the back and pecks on the cheek can be shared before the reception and dancing commence. And Tommy is just lucky enough to notice the bride and the groom sharing a quiet moment on the edge of the rooftop.

He's thinking of songs that sum up these two. There will be several that go on this video, and of course they'll be songs that both Dan and Skylar love. Skylar's a country girl, so there will have to be a Blake Shelton song, and maybe one from her favorite band, Thompson Square. Dan, of course, loves his classic rock. So there will be something loud and epic in the video. Led Zeppelin or Aerosmith or Fleetwood Mac. But the songs Tommy's thinking about are the cuts for moments like this, with the two of them talking and smiling and expressing something only they will know.

Skylar looks lost. *"Lost in Love,"* Tommy jokes with himself. The bride is smiling and staring up at Dan while the groom seems to be searching for words.

He looks like he's trying to tell her something important.

Tommy imagines a slow, romantic ballad playing at this moment. Maybe a sultry Norah Jones song. That certainly would fit her lost look. The backdrop of the small city and the endless sky behind the gorgeous couple make this a great shot.

Dan's face is earnest, and he seems to need to get something off his chest. But then a figure comes over to them and interrupts this moment. It's Lauren, hugging Skylar and then Dan. Tommy doesn't have to be a mind reader or lip reader to know Lauren's telling them how much she loves them.

Music begins to blare out of the reception hall.

"They want the wedding party inside now," Allison shouts out to them.

Tommy shuts off the camera and follows Allison inside. The story of his life.

The song introducing them is an inside joke between Dan and Skylar. The first time they met, Dan made a reference to the two of them going out, to which Skylar replied, "Don't stop believing." Dan soon began requesting the Journey song anytime Skylar was around. The first time they danced was at a bar after Dan played the song on a jukebox. Now the same music plays over the speakers in the reception area while the bridal party is introduced.

They sit at a straight line of tables facing the rest of the wedding goers. The music soon fades out, and the DJ asks for the maid of honor. It's time for the toast, and Tommy makes sure he's recording.

Allison stands up and faces Skylar.

"Okay, well, I promise all of you I'm not going to repeat what happened last night," Allison says with a reassuring smile. "Sky and I are more like sisters than friends. We—we've been best friends—BFFs—"

"Garfield Elementary," Skylar shouts.

"Woot woot," Lauren calls out.

The crowd responds with smiles and some laughter. Allison appears a bit more at ease hearing it. "Can you believe it? Friends since sixth grade. Garfield Elementary. That's right: 1999."

Someone from the audience shouts that they're old. Allison pauses for a moment and gives a mock-sinister stare. "That summer Skylar made me go to her church camp, and we made her try her first cigarette—"

"And last," Skylar makes sure to tell everybody.

"I can't tell you what Skylar and Dan and these people mean to me," Allison says, gesturing to Lauren and then

Jack and Tommy. "I could try, but I promised you I wouldn't get too emotional. All I know is that I've never seen Skylar look more joyful and more beautiful than she does right now."

Allison holds up her wineglass. "Please raise your glasses and wish my best friend Skylar and her amazing husband a fulfilling and prosperous future together. I'm so happy for you guys."

The crowd gives them a loud round of cheers, then drinks to Skylar and Dan. Tommy moves the camera to Jack as he stands up and walks over to get the mike from Allison. He puts a familiar arm around her and kisses her in routine fashion. Then he faces the audience and gives them a smile. Tommy knows Jack's dangerous behind a microphone.

"It only makes sense that I'm the best man, seeing as I'm responsible for setting up these two fine folks. Can I get a round of applause?"

Tommy chuckles, wondering if Jack wants the claps for the couple or for himself. It's almost surely the latter.

"That's right, I'll take the credit," Jack hams it up. "So Dan calls me and tells me he's going to ask Skylar to marry him, and only one thing went through my mind: I'm a pretty good matchmaker."

The crowd loves it. Tommy can't help smiling at his buddy.

"But really, I'll never forget what Dan said. 'When you find the one person—whether you believe in God or fate or whatever—when your path crosses that one person's, you act on it.' And you did, Dan. So I say congrats to you two today for doing just that and making it real."

Jack toasts them and the rest of the crowd yells out, "Cheers!" as Tommy pans over to Dan and Skylar and then past them to Allison. He notices her serious expression as she sips from her glass and then puts it on the table, looking down for a moment. Looking lost in some kind of thought.

Tommy doesn't need to wonder what she's thinking. He can read her mind.

He's been able to for quite a long time.

"I want to say a few words," Dan says as he takes Skylar's hands and walks over to where Jack's standing.

The groom gives his best man a hug before taking the mike. Jack moves next to Tommy, who's still filming.

"This is the greatest day of my life," Dan says as he puts his arm around Skylar and holds her close. "Of *our* lives. I only wish my parents were still here to see how happy you've made me, Skylar. But I'm thankful to be surrounded by the greatest friends . . . and I'm beyond undeserving to have the most beautiful bride in the history of the world. I am one lucky man."

The crowd applauds as *awwws* can be heard from several people. Tommy turns the camera to Jack.

"Dude, our boy is cheesy," Tommy says. "'In the history of the world'? Come on."

Jack just pushes the camera back on the couple in the

spotlight. Skylar takes the microphone and speaks softly into it. "Dad, can you say the prayer?"

Mr. Chapman stands and doesn't bother with the mike since he has such a strong and deep voice. "Let's bow our heads in prayer."

Everybody does. Everybody, of course, except for Tommy. He moves the camera and suddenly finds it stuck on a familiar figure. For a moment, he just stays focused on her without anybody else noticing. She doesn't know and neither does Jack. Nobody does. And this is the way it's been for quite some time.

"Father, we thank You for Skylar and Dan and the gift they are to all of us."

I'd never know You if it weren't for Skylar and Dan.

"We ask You to bless them and keep them close to You."

And keep us all close together too.

"We thank You for all the family and friends who have traveled to be here today."

Especially close friends.

Allison opens her eyes before Mr. Chapman finishes. She looks directly into the camera, directly at Tommy. He jerks the camera back to Skylar's father.

"We ask all of this in Your Son's name. Amen."

Tommy stops recording for a moment.

"I'm starving," Jack says, heading back to sit down.

For a second, Tommy glances at Allison again, but she's talking and laughing with Lauren. Busy and oblivious and as beautiful as the bride. Just like always.

When the dancing commences, Tommy is still filming, sometimes from the side of the dance floor and sometimes right in the middle of it. The DJ has obviously been briefed by Skylar; all the songs are perfect. It's a great combo of fun songs every wedding reception should have combined with some of the favorites the gang loved when they were all hanging out in college.

The real fun starts in the middle of Dan and Skylar's official first dance, set to a slow song. Without warning, the song seems to break, a hip-hop number starts, and Skylar begins to dance alone. Lauren rushes to join in. Dan shakes his head and laughs at his crazy wife.

Tommy puts the camera down for a moment when the Bee Gees' "Stayin' Alive" comes on. He goes into the center of the throng and does his best bit of moving and shaking. It's not John Travolta quality but it's still fun and that's the point. Dan and Skylar are out there, swinging and bobbing and laughing all the while.

Barry Gibb's shrill falsetto rolls across the dance floor singing about the city breakin' and everybody shakin', but he's a-stayin' alive, thank you very much. The floor is packed and they're all laughing and sweating to the tune. The only one Tommy doesn't see is Allison.

I think I need to go find where she's at.

When the song ends and a tune that was popular around the time they graduated starts playing, Tommy finds the camera and heads out in search of the maid of honor. He gets a drink first and notices a tall brunette in the short, shapely dress. Actually, it's her legs that he notices first, but he tries not to be too obvious as he smiles and says hello to her.

"Are you the videographer or something?" she asks as she stirs the drink she just ordered from the bar in the corner of the room.

She's got a sexy Southern drawl to her voice, a sweet sound that seems friendly to the whole world.

"Documentarian. I'm doing this as a favor to Dan. I was his wingman throughout college. Name's Tommy."

"Ashton," she says, shaking his hand and giving him a very friendly smile. "Nice to meet you."

"Cool. I'll find you on Facebook."

The smile stays with her as she walks off. Tommy can't help but watch her as she disappears into the crowd of minglers and dancers. When he turns he notices Lauren standing at his side.

"She's taken, Tommy."

He lets out a sigh and a laugh. "Story of my life."

7 MIRRORS

Lauren feels lighter, brighter, and somehow better.

Maybe the worry was simply the enemy wanting to bring her down. To cast a shadow on a special day for one of her closest friends. She doesn't know. She simply knows her two good friends look happy and radiant, and they're together. They're linked together and hopefully, with God's help and maybe the help of some others as well, they'll stay locked together forever.

She thinks about a Bible passage that she read recently about worry: *"So don't worry about tomorrow, for tomorrow will bring its own worries. Today's trouble is enough for today."*

There's something comforting about knowing the Bible

isn't saying that today will be free from hurts and suffering and discomfort. It simply says to dwell on the day you have. To deal with it and let tomorrow be.

She's tried to do that even though it's hard. When you're someone who likes to have control, this world can often resemble staring into a broken mirror. You see the sharp, ragged edges but lose sight of yourself.

"Somebody isn't dancing," Skylar calls out from behind her.

Lauren turns and sees the bride approaching. "Oh my goodness," Lauren says.

"What? My eyeliner running or something?"

"No. I actually see—let me count them—two, three, no . . . four beads of sweat on your forehead. I can't believe it."

"Stop."

"You're a real person who actually *sweats*."

"And you're crazy," Skylar tells her. "We gotta get you back out there to bust a move. We all know who the real dancer is."

"I'm just saving my moves for later. It's gonna be a long night."

Skylar nods, then finds an untouched glass of water on a nearby table to sip. "It's a bit surreal, isn't it?"

"What is?"

"This moment. Having all these people here. It's like some last hurrah."

Lauren looks out at the crowd. "Or maybe it's the first

hurrah. You know? The start of something bigger and better."

Skylar gives her a big hug. "I'm so glad to know you, girlfriend," Sky tells her.

"Feeling is mutual. You know that."

"I do."

Skylar takes her hand.

"What? Where are we going?"

"You are gonna stop watching and start moving."

A favorite song begins to play and Lauren finally stops resisting.

Soon the music and the motion and the moving lights all make Lauren laugh and feel like there's no reason to worry about tomorrow.

Tomorrow will take care of itself.

Today is what matters.

Being here in the moment.

Thank You, God. Thanks for moments like this.

A dark world only makes the brighter moments shine that much more.

8
THE END IS NEAR

The feeling is back, and it couldn't have come at a worse time.

In the midst of the loud music and laughter and flowing gowns and sparkling smiles, Allison sits at a table tapping the edge of her champagne glass. She watches Dan and Skylar cut the cake and then perform for the audience. Dan acts like he's going to shove some in Skylar's face, but Allison knows there's a better chance of the sky falling than cake getting on the bride tonight. The couple flirt and playfully nibble at the desert while cameras and cell phones take pictures.

Allison feels restless.

The confusion and anger bubble up inside her, and she knows there's no way to fight it. She can't forget, not here and now. This whole day is about marriage and happily-ever-afters. It's the thing she's waited for and wanted for a long time. The nagging voice in the back of her heart sounds louder now, and it's demanding some kind of action. It doesn't want to hide in the shadows anymore.

How long am I going to be sitting here on the sidelines?

It's not like she isn't happy for Dan and Skylar. She's overjoyed for them. But she's also jealous and impatient. She knows she'd look just as good wearing a bride's dress and dancing with her groom and cutting the cake and being the center of attention. But that's just the superficial part of it all.

I want someone by my side to grow old with.

The problem is, the voice of doubt that's been nagging her is asking her whether the man who will be at her side is Jack. *Of course it is,* she has answered herself time and time again. *He's everything I want and need, and I love him,* she's tried to tell herself. But somehow the voice seems to know her too well. The voice keeps asking her to stop wasting time and stop wanting something that might not happen.

She and Jack have had conversations about it, certainly. She's joked with him until the joke has become more painful than anything else. She's tried to ask the question that everybody else is asking, but it seems too real and far too raw.

I shouldn't have to ask that question. I should be the one being asked.

The question of when. When is it going to happen? When will it be time? When will that day come when Jack finally asks her whether she wants to be with him for the rest of their lives? When will the dream come true for them?

"This is pretty awesome," a familiar voice says as he takes a seat beside her and sets a plate in front of her. "Cake for the girl at table 1?"

Allison smiles at Tommy. "Is it diet?"

"You have to be done starving yourself. The wedding's over."

She glances at the large sliver of cake with all its delicious, white, fatty frosting. A part of Allison wants to grab a chunk of the wedding cake with both hands and just start chowing down. Then with a mouthful of cake she could give Jack the bad news.

You could have had me when I was thin but that time is done and I'm just not gonna care anymore.

Allison slides the plate over and takes a bite. "Wow. This is good."

The music begins again, this time slowing down as couples unite on the dance floor. Allison sees Skylar's parents dancing together and sharing a moment. Mr. Chapman looks down at his wife with a glance Allison can only dream of getting one day. She doesn't know how long the two of them have been married, but that's what she wants. Being there with her best friend years down the road and still being able to receive that look. A look of pride and happiness and, most of all, a look full of belonging. "They're so cute."

"Come on," Tommy says as he leans his head over to get her attention. "I've seen you in action at weddings before, and currently you're not dancing on a table or breaking glasses, so . . . hey, Allie. It's me. What's up?"

She sighs. "It's my best friend's wedding and I'm upset because my boyfriend just gave a speech about how important it is to 'act on it' when you cross paths with the right person."

For a moment, Tommy doesn't say anything.

'Cause he knows I'm right.

"I thought it was a pretty good speech," he says.

"I crossed paths with Jack nearly seven years ago. *Seven.*"

"I get it." Tommy's trademark mischievous grin spreads across his face. "Always a bridesmaid, never—"

"A bride. Yeah, yeah. I'm lame, huh?"

"No. You're a catch, Allie, and the most amazing woman I've ever met."

For a moment, she only shakes her head and looks at him to see whether he's joking. But the sarcastic tone is gone. The wry smile is gone too. He's being sincere.

"What? Why the skeptical look?" he asks. "At least top one hundred for sure."

"Funny."

"I'm still thinking probably number one."

Allison wants to say something but she's not sure what.

He's encouraging her like always, and she knows she sometimes takes it for granted. But still, it feels good and sometimes it's necessary in moments like this. Just to have someone who gets it. Who gets her.

A funky dance track begins to play, and Tommy surprises her by taking her hand. "Come on—this is a celebration." He pulls her to her feet.

Soon all six of them are dancing side by side, singing the song they all know so well. Allison forgets about her doubts and that nagging voice. Right now her friends are surrounding her and the noise is drowning out anything else. Jack is smiling by her side, and she takes his hand. Soon Skylar has her other hand.

She glances around for Tommy but can't see him. He was just here; he must be somewhere nearby. Probably filming the rest of them or something like that.

Then the music takes over and she follows Tommy's advice and keeps celebrating.

Over twenty-five women stand on the dance floor facing Skylar. It's the bouquet toss, and Lauren almost had to drag her out here to get her to participate. It's so obvious, so clichéd. Everybody wants the maid of honor to catch it, right? She's the chosen one. It's her turn. She's the one who's going to get married next. *Allison and Jack. Jack and Allison. When's the date? How's he going to propose?*

"I'm not catching that," Allison says to Lauren.

"Oh, stop."

A couple of girls stand in front of Allison, and that's fine. She wanders off to the side of the group.

"One," Skylar shouts out.

Some of these ladies actually seem to want to catch it.

"Two."

Allison looks over at Lauren, who is laughing. She only shakes her head.

"Three!"

Skylar doesn't toss it over her head but rather turns and flips the bouquet her direction.

No way.

A couple of women go for it but it lands in the center of Allison's chest like a baseball in a catcher's mitt. The crowd roars as her hands desperately want to let go. Yet she can't. She smiles and then lifts up the bouquet. Skylar is beaming and laughing.

She's gonna pay for that.

The bride rushes over and gives her a big hug.

"I'm going to kill you," Allison says.

"Where's Jack?" Skylar asks, looking all around. "Get him out here."

Allison knows Jack is sitting at a table at the edge of the dance floor, watching and drinking a beer and remaining far enough away. He looks uncomfortable when Skylar calls attention to him. Skylar doesn't see him yet but she's calling out for him to come onto the dance floor. Allison is still smiling and expects Jack to come to her side.

But something else happens instead.

Something nobody else sees.

Jack rolls his eyes and stands up, then slips away into the back of the room.

For a second, Allison feels as if she's been punched in the gut. She didn't *want* to catch the bouquet, but Skylar had other plans. But seeing this . . . especially after the words he just spoke . . .

The hyper, too-cool-for-school DJ comes over with his mike and large voice and corny smile. "And who does this lovely lady belong to? Looks like somebody else is getting hitched soon!"

Allison almost takes the bouquet and swats the Justin Timberlake wannabe over the head with it. Skylar has an arm around her and is still looking for Jack.

"I know he's here," the DJ says. "I just saw him a few minutes ago."

All Allison wants to do is leave the bouquet and this bridesmaid dress and the banquet hall behind. The image of the bridge fills her mind again.

I should've known. Should've expected this. Should've assumed things would be this way.

Moments later, Allison glances up at the sky on the empty rooftop deck. The chairs and the floral altar are still there. She leans against the edge of the wall and closes her eyes, picturing a sweet moment from the ceremony.

She sees a father lifting one of the two-year-old ring bearers up to the tree. The young girl holds an envelope in her hand, one that surely contains money. She places it on the tree, where other envelopes hang. A gift for the future. A gift of life. A simple gift.

This makes Allison think of her own father. Her parents divorced when she was sixteen. The term *sweet sixteen* will always leave a sour taste in her mouth.

"There you are."

She opens her eyes and sees Jack.

"I've been looking for you. Where'd you go?"

"I've been pretty easy to find today," she says.

Jack looks puzzled. "What's wrong?"

She breathes in, wondering if she's going to do this right now. She knows it's not the right place or time.

But there's never going to be a right place and a right time and a right moment and a right man to ask the right question for the right purpose. Right?

"I gotta go," she says, looking away from him.

Jack seems not to understand if she's talking about leaving the outside rooftop or leaving the wedding reception altogether. Frankly, Allison isn't sure either.

"Why?" he asks. "What happened?"

"It doesn't matter."

"What? Tell me."

He moves closer to her, innocent eyes looking down at her. The kind that would melt any girl's heart. The problem is they've melted hers far too many times. And each time it hardens again, it takes a slightly different shape. Now her heart is misshapen and simply worn out.

"I love you, and I show it. But I'm baffled, Jack. Either you don't love me or you have a really lousy way of letting me know it."

His shirt is partly unbuttoned, his tie unknotted and hanging there like a noose around his neck. He looks wounded.

"What happened?"

"I saw you roll your eyes."

Now he gets it.

"Look, I'm sorry—"

He moves to embrace her but she pushes him away. "I don't want to do this anymore."

Jack lets out a sigh. "Come on, Allie. I love you. You know that. We've been together for five years—"

"Seven."

He tries again to move closer and touch her. That always works and that's always her downfall. They'll argue and they'll begin to talk about serious things and then he'll embrace her and settle in for silence. For unspoken words. But not this time. Not anymore. She begins to walk away.

She reaches the doors to head inside when he grabs her hand.

"Don't leave," he says.

But she does. She waits for the elevator and when the doors open, Tommy walks out, carrying a grin and his camera. He begins filming without even noticing that they're arguing.

"Really, Tommy?" Jack asks.

"What? What's going on?"

Allison slips into the elevator and the doors begin to shut. Jack calls her name but it's not enough. It's too late.

She knows the end has finally arrived. Soon enough everybody else will know it too.

9
TAKE A DEEP BREATH

Tommy asks the obvious after Allison is gone. "She upset?"

It's not the first time Tommy has walked in on something going on between Jack and Allison, but today something feels different.

The thumping bass back in the banquet room is the only thing he can hear for a moment. It seems like Jack is thinking, though Tommy has no idea what he's thinking about. Jack is seldom lost for words and almost never lost in thought. Jack doesn't wade in those kinds of deep waters.

"She just needs to cool off a little bit. Then we'll have a talk. She's just heated." He brushes back his hair, the hesitation still there. "C'mon," he says to Tommy. "Let's go back."

"You sure?"

"Yeah. I'm sure. Of course I'm sure. This is a party. Let's go."

The two friends, looking like twins in their gray suits, head back in to the party. Tommy's not going to pry any more with Jack even though his buddy sounds doubtful. It sounded like Jack was telling himself that he's sure, but nothing about his tone made it seem like he really is.

They enter the busy and loud room without Allison. She'll surely show back up in a while.

"You want something to drink?" Jack asks Tommy.

Tommy nods. "Yeah, whatever you're having."

As Jack wanders off toward the bar, Tommy slips out his cell phone. The screen saver shows the movie poster of *Apocalypse Now* but no text message. As Bruno Mars belts the dancers into shape on the floor in the center of the room, Tommy types out a text. Just to see what's up with Allison.

He sees Jack waving a beer and goes over to him. Soon enough Jack and Allison will be smiling and hanging all over each other again. This is the pattern like always, with Tommy right in the center of it. Always trying to help out.

The camera is rolling again.

Tommy feels the elevator they're in moving up as he points the video recorder at Mr. and Mrs. Chapman.

"Thank you for coming to our room to drop off some of the wedding presents," Skylar's father says, his gray hair looking as perfect as it did when Tommy saw him a few hours ago.

"No problem. Now that I have you trapped—what's the secret to staying married all these years?"

"I'm always right," Mrs. Chapman says.

"That's actually correct," Mr. Chapman says quickly with a smile.

They're a good-looking couple, especially Mrs. Chapman. Tommy can tell Skylar gets her dominant genes from her mother, who looks attractive in her evening dress showing off a trim figure. The Chapmans laugh at each other, and it's a moment that Tommy loves capturing on video. Tommy knows *this* is one of the secrets.

Keep laughing together. Keep the humor coming.

Mr. Chapman clears his throat and looks directly into the camera.

"Skylar, if you are watching this right now, your wedding was absolutely beautiful."

"You know your daughter wouldn't have it any other way," Tommy adds.

"It should have been at the church," Mrs. Chapman says.

"It was her choice," Mr. Chapman gently assures. "Even if it's not what we wanted."

"And we all know Skylar gets what she wants," Tommy jokes.

"Like mother like—"

Mr. Chapman pauses. Tommy blinks several times, thinking he's not seeing the right image on the camera screen.

It looks like I can see their breath. As if we're standing outside on a cold winter day.

The elevator seems to be stopped. Just like Tommy's breathing. Just like his pulse.

He glances at the couple he's facing and sees something awful. Noticing their breath is one thing. It's odd, but it's not just that. They both suddenly look pale as ghosts, as if they've both seen something horrific.

"Did you feel that?" Mr. Chapman asks his wife.

"It just got so cold," she says.

Tommy is confused; he doesn't feel any change. *What is happening here?*

Mr. Chapman turns to look at Tommy and his camera. The look is empty. As if any feeling or emotion or love or anything is all gone. Absent. Boom. Just vanished. And something else—his pupils suddenly start getting smaller.

Tommy is about to say something when he's interrupted. The elevator jolts as Skylar's parents fall to the carpeted floor and land in awkward poses with loud thuds.

This is not happening this has gotta be a joke right right?

Tommy tilts the camera down and sees their lifeless faces looking up at him. He knows in an instant this isn't a joke. They're dead, both of them, just like that. He can just feel it. He knows.

The camera drops to the floor and lands near Mrs. Chapman's head as Tommy leans over and calls out their names and tries to revive them. They're so cold, both of them. The temperature hasn't changed, but they feel like they've been stored in an ice locker for a week.

A rush of searing, shaking terror fills Tommy.

"Mr. Chapman, Mrs. Chapman. You guys. Come on."

He moves them, then jerks them, then actually slaps them but he gets nothing. As he picks up his camera, he sees the whitewashed, empty face of Skylar's mother. Her pupils are the size of pinpricks, as if she's just been staring into some bright light for a long time.

He screams for help and keeps screaming, the sound of his voice actually assuring him that he's not dead or losing his mind. This isn't a joke. Even the fun-loving Chapmans wouldn't do something like this. They look and feel dead.

And I'm trapped with them.

"Somebody help me," he cries out as he feels the elevator moving again.

His arms and legs are shivering as the door finally opens. For a second Tommy wonders what to do with the bodies sprawled out on the floor.

Then he hears the screams coming from the wedding reception.

He doesn't hesitate. He bolts out of the elevator and down the hall.

He has no idea what kind of nightmare he's about to see. But it sounds worse than the terror he just witnessed.

As he rushes toward the horrible sounds, he thinks of one thing.

Allison.

10
SANCTUARY

Allison wants to pray but can't. She sits in the pew in a silent and empty church with the glowing colors of the stained-glass windows on each side filling the room with a sky-blue sort of light. This place gives her a modicum of hope. It's a bit like going window shopping and seeing the amazing and expensive fashions all nearly within reach. If-onlys fill her soul. If only she had the money to buy that dress. If only she had the motivation to blurt out the prayer she's held for some time.

If only.

This isn't the first time she's come to Rivertown Community Church. Since living around Wilmington the last few years, she's occasionally found herself walking back from a bar or a night out and then wandering in here. There was the time Jack had too much to drink and she left him being obnoxious with the rest of their friends. Another time was on a night when he was supposed to meet her but ended up canceling because of work. There was even the evening after Skylar's bridal shower when Allison just slipped inside here to think.

There's a calm here that's comforting. She has her phone silenced and she's not checking Facebook or Twitter or Instagram. The news of the day isn't getting to her. Nobody from the wedding party is intruding with their witty comments or deep thoughts or probing questions.

It's just her and . . .

God?

She can't say that exactly. She thinks maybe it's something like that but it's not like she comes here to pray. She's not at that point. She's warming up to the concept. Getting the seat in the pew warm. Getting used to the idea of staring at a cross and looking upward.

All she can think is what she should do now. And how she's wasted all these years. And how she needs to start fresh.

Tomorrow can be a better day.

A hundred different ideas and thoughts flood her. Then she hears a violent crash outside that jerks her up out of the padded pew. A car alarm goes off and she hears a scream.

Another scream, this time from somewhere back in the church. It's a large church that extends for a whole block.

"Help me!"

This is a woman's voice from outside.

Another alarm sounds. Another crash. A door slamming. The ground underneath her shaking.

What is happening?

She glances up at the cross one more time, then heads through the doors at the front of the church, toward where the sound of the crash came from. When she opens the door, she finds a car rammed into another. One of the cars doesn't seem to have anybody inside it. A woman sits in the other car's driver's seat bleeding from her head. The car door hangs open. The woman sees Allison and says something and then tries to get out of the car. She crumples to the street.

Allison rushes over to help her.

She hears screaming in the background. Someone yelling. A man runs past on the sidewalk. There's the sound of glass breaking. Another car flies by them and nearly crashes as it veers around and keeps tearing down the road.

"What happened?" Allison says as she helps the woman stand.

There is a deep gash in the woman's forehead that's gushing blood. The woman holds a hand up to stop it but that's only smearing it everywhere.

"The car just suddenly started coming toward me. There was no driver. It hit me going thirty miles an hour."

"Let's get you to the grass over here," she tells the woman, who's probably in her fifties. "Let me see if anybody is in the other car."

There's an explosion somewhere nearby that makes Allison duck instinctively. She looks at the sky and it seems different, as if gray clouds were suddenly painted there with the touch of a button like on a phone app.

It didn't look like that when I entered the church.

She peers into the other car and sees a figure draped across the front seats.

She opens the door slowly. "Hello? Are you okay? Hello, sir?"

It's a heavyset man in shorts and a T-shirt. She can see the side of his face. She leans over.

Then she touches his skin and feels the cold. His eyes aren't moving and his profile looks like a wax dummy's.

He must've had a heart attack or something while driving.

Allison goes back over to the woman sitting on the grass looking like she might have a concussion.

A tall black man in khakis and a button-down shirt runs toward them screaming. "They're dead all of them are dead they're all dead and we're next we're going to be next."

Allison moves off the sidewalk and expects the terrified man to stop but he doesn't. He's sweaty and out of breath but he moves past them yelling and cursing and sprinting toward somewhere.

In the distance something is burning. Allison can see black smoke coming from behind the trees.

"Let's go back in the church, okay?" she tells the woman.

She checks her phone but there are no new messages. She tries to make a call but there's no service.

The worst thing she could do is flip out like the guy running past them just did.

Another explosion tears through the afternoon air and makes her wince. She looks around and for a second can't even think.

Get inside go inside and get away from whatever is happening out here. Help the woman and get back in the church.

Allison starts to say something and then realizes she hasn't taken a breath in a few moments. She breathes in and clears her throat, then leans over and helps the bleeding woman to her feet.

"Let's go inside and find something to stop the bleeding. Then we'll call the police and figure out what's happening."

A siren sounds in the distance. There are unfamiliar noises everywhere. She sees a dog scrambling down the road, a bit like the man who just passed them. Frantic, out of breath, going who knows where.

Allison thinks of the gang she left behind at the hotel. Now she wishes she had stayed with them.

I have to get ahold of them somehow. Or get back to the hotel.

She knows this isn't just something happening on the side of this street. All over Wilmington, some kind of dark chaos is occurring. She pictures Jack and Tommy and Skylar and Dan and Lauren.

Then she thinks of her family.

"Come on," she finally says, snapping herself out of it.

They head back into the church. Maybe they'll find some kind of sanctuary inside.

11
GONE

Death fills the floor.

The seconds move by like falling sledgehammers dropping against his soul. It's too much to take in, yet his eyes and his ears are forced to see and hear all of it. Every awful little bit.

Tommy stumbles over a body as he makes his way to the reception room. This looks like a battleground, like some kind of national tragedy just took place on the top floor of the Plantation Hotel. Yet there is no gun-toting crazy person to be found. No bleeding wounds to be seen. No visible remnants of a bomb blast.

But death is all around him.

There are gasps and screams and moans and mumbling. Shouts of all kinds. Too many to make sense of. The music is still playing, making things even worse. The driving dance track by Lady Gaga only adds to the utter hysteria.

I'm never gonna listen to that song again without picturing all of this.

Not that he can afford to worry about ever listening to music again.

He's gotta survive this right now.

The inside of the banquet room devastates him. Bodies are everywhere, dropped and discarded like a scene from a ransacked mannequin warehouse. Figures are draped over the fallen, crying and calling and freaking out. He sees trays of food and broken glasses littering the floor. As he walks in hoping to find someone he knows, he can hear the crinkle of glass under his dress shoes.

His eyes land on an overturned table near the front that had held a bunch of framed photographs of Dan and Skylar. They're now all spread over the ground as if they've been trampled.

People are running around and the sounds of screams are everywhere.

What kind of hell is happening in front of me?

For a second everything goes on pause, including the sights and the sounds and his brain. He feels like he is moving in slow motion until another voice pokes him awake.

Don't fade out now just act and react.

He instinctively cries out Jack's name because he needs

some help here. He moves in and sees mangled legs in high heels beside an overturned table. Tommy sees the face and the hair and knows this woman.

It's the Southern belle he was talking to at the bar. He notices the cross pendant hanging around her neck, then sees the blank expression similar to the one the Chapmans had.

She's not moving, not breathing, not alive in any way.

"What the—?" He can't say more.

A funny and sad and weird thought comes to him. He thinks of the last episode of *The Walking Dead* he saw and for a second he wonders if he needs to grab some kind of weapon. But that's why it's funny and sad. This isn't a zombie movie, and these people aren't coming back from the dead.

"Dan? Sky?" Tommy's eyes scan through the blurry motion and then see the white bridal dress moving around. Skylar is up and moving and that's a good thing. She's hovering over someone, trying to revive them.

Then Tommy sees Jack nearby and darts over to him.

"Jack—man—Skylar's parents in the elevator—they just fell down dead—and this—what just happened?"

His mind is moving so fast he can't even finish whole sentences. Jack looks like he's in a slow-motion daze himself.

"I don't know, Tommy," Jack says as his eyes look all around them. "I don't know. . . ."

Two voices rush up to them. Tommy sees Dan's pale face and Skylar's wide eyes.

"Lauren's dead," are the only words he hears Skylar say.

She's dead?

He thinks of the figure Skylar was just hovering over and knows it has to be Lauren.

She can't be gone.

"I'm looking for my mom and dad," Skylar says through tears.

Tommy thinks of his own parents and his sister. Then of Lauren and of the end of last summer when she told him she thought something bad was going to happen, how she kept dreaming about it.

"Have you seen my parents?"

Tommy hears Skylar but can't answer, can't even look at her.

"I can't find them anywhere."

He feels numb and just wants to close his eyes to this and to everything.

"Tommy?"

Jack is looking at him. Skylar's waiting for an answer. Dan looks scared.

"Come on, man," Jack says.

It seems like only five seconds ago Dan and Skylar were saying their vows. It seems like they were only another five seconds away from leaving to go on their honeymoon. But now this.

Now Tommy has to tell her the truth.

"I'm so sorry, Sky. I was with them in the elevator and they just—"

The bride crumbles to the floor, ignoring her dress and

her makeup and anything else as she bursts into fresh tears. Dan goes to her side, cradling her with his arm.

"I just want to go see them," she cries out between sobs. "Now."

Jack looks at Tommy and seems to realize something. "Allison," he says.

Skylar is on her feet again and sprints out of the room with Dan following. Jack pulls out his phone as an elderly woman behind them starts screaming at a high pitch.

"Cell service is busy," Jack says.

An explosion shakes the building and causes both Jack and Tommy to hunker down as if it's in the room. Audible gasps and moans are heard as everybody realizes the boom came from outside.

"That sounded like a missile," Tommy says to Jack. "Come on; let's see what's happening outside."

Nothing in him wants to go out and see where the blast came from, but then again, nothing in him wants to remain in this open grave of a room.

Tommy and Jack head toward the glass doors of the balcony, unsure what awaits them.

The air outside feels thick while the sky looks even thicker. Angry clouds cover it only moments after it was a clear, open window up to heaven. Tommy feels a gust of wind and sees figures already scattered on the rooftop deck, looking out at the chaos around them. He pushes past a couple he saw talking to the Chapmans. The woman is crying while the man consoles her. Tommy walks up to the edge of the rooftop and stares out over the city.

Columns of smoke rise from the buildings below. Dozens of different noises try to tackle him down. Sirens and car horns and muffled voices and screams sound from everywhere. Tommy watches in disbelief. There's nothing he can think. It's all too real, too horrible, too raw.

He sees a balding man with an arm around a woman who might be his wife on a rooftop across from him. Tommy can see their expressions. Bleak, scared, empty. They look his way as if waiting to see how he can help.

They all seem so helpless. So alone. Is that how he looks too?

Behind the couple, something explodes, followed by a large smoke plume resembling a thought bubble. Tommy can imagine the words that would fill it.

Many of them would be curse words.

Tommy looks down at the street and sees the jam of cars. People are running everywhere like ants fleeing a boot pounding down on them.

This can't be happening.

A scary droning sound comes from the sky, and Tommy looks up, half expecting to find alien invaders. Yet it's only a plane flying.

Only a plane. Flying dangerously low. Flying—

The plane slams into the rooftop across the way that held the huddled elderly couple. A series of groans and cries and curses follow. Tommy ducks and dives to the floor and hears yet another booming sound.

For a second he's kneeling and about to get up when the whole world starts to shake. His camera slides as he tries to grab onto something but there's nothing around.

The violent jerking lasts a few moments, then stops. And then the panicked chaos really commences.

12
STRANGERS

For a moment, Allison steps out of time and finds herself wading in a pool full of memories.

The cold water of the creek against bone-white feet. The trail through the woods. The log cabin.

She still remembers.

The tiny church on the corner with the endless steeple and the cross on top. The smiles. The pastor with the round, bald head. The coffee cakes after the sermon.

She still sees them.

Strangers surrounding us. Prayers. Unfamiliar words full of hope. Words clearly foreign to skeptical parents.

Allison still hears them.

The words. So brief. During a dark period when Mom and Dad needed something else. Something more. But nothing more came. And we never went back.

"Miss?"

Allison turns and sees the older woman from the car accident standing next to her. The look on her face says it all. Eyes almost bulging with disbelief. No color. So grave and hard and anxious.

"Are you okay?" the woman asks her.

Allison is standing by a sink in a small bathroom down the hall from the sanctuary. She's been standing here for some time, thinking, trying to figure out what's happening, hearing the noises continuing to go off in the distance. It sounds like a war is happening in the city of Wilmington. Yet she can't even call out or access Internet on her phone to find out who exactly is fighting whom.

"Yeah." Allison turns off the bathroom light. "How's your head?"

"I'm glad you found a bandage. I'm still woozy."

"You probably shouldn't be walking around."

"I didn't want to be left alone in there," the woman says. "I keep hearing things."

"I don't know what's going on outside."

"No . . ." The woman stares at her for a minute, then looks around them. "I'm talking about noises from inside this church."

Allison nods. She doesn't know her way around the building. She has only ever stepped foot through the main doors and into the sanctuary.

"Let's try to find a kitchen, okay? Maybe get you something to drink."

"I don't think they have what I want."

Allison looks at the woman and sees the slight hint of a smile coming on. She chuckles and introduces herself. "I'm Allison."

"I'm Beverly. Bev. Thank you for helping me."

"Of course."

"You look all pretty and made-up. Were you going somewhere tonight?"

"My best friend got married today."

"At this church?"

Allison shakes her head. "No. The Plantation Hotel a few blocks away."

She knows this only fills Beverly with more questions. Before being able to answer any of them, they hear someone crying down the hallway. It's a manic sort of wailing.

"Come on," Allison tells Beverly as she heads toward the noise.

"They just dropped dead, all of them, right in the middle of the meeting."

The bodies in the conference room haven't been touched. A man is plopped over a long conference table, his head sideways and his mouth open. Another man is lifeless in his chair, staring upward with arms hanging down. A woman is hunched halfway out of her armchair. The eyes—the ones they can see—all have the same blank look.

The guy built like a football player wiping tears off his face hasn't told them his name or what else happened. When Allison and Beverly found him in the room, standing by the wall looking at the dead bodies and just crying, they made sure he was okay. He can't seem to leave the room. He's too scared to do anything but watch the corpses, as if they might come back to life.

"But how did they all die, just like that?" Beverly asks, looking up close at the man resting against the table.

"I don't know." The survivor continues his silent crying and they can hear his quick, distraught breaths. "I just don't know."

Allison keeps distance between herself and the big guy. She keeps looking for something strange, something that might have been used on these people. *Did he kill them?* Something just doesn't make sense. Three people don't just die on the spot like this. Especially when there's someone else in the room left alive. That would rule out something like poison or toxic air. Then again she doesn't know what to rule out. Right now she has to assume anything is possible.

"They're dead all right," Beverly says.

The guy wipes sweat from his forehead and keeps rubbing as if doing so will make a genie appear.

"Let's just leave them here and get some help."

"I've been trying to call but I can't get anybody," the man says. "Phones are dead. Do you guys—?"

"I tried mine and same thing," Allison says.

Beverly shakes her head, the wrinkles on her face standing out in the light. "Mine is in the car. But I assume it's probably the same. It's not one of those smartphones, just an old-fashioned cell phone."

"Let's just try and see who else we can—"

Everything suddenly starts shaking. Not slowly but fast. Allison sways as the ceiling panels shudder and then drop. The lights go out and she hears Beverly scream and the man say an earthquake is happening.

Allison falls to the ground and covers her head and all she can think is that she's going to die in this dark room surrounded by strangers.

And there's nothing she can do about it.

13
TERROR

Sirens are going off, either in the distance or in his head. Tommy isn't sure. He's just moving, following Jack, trying to make it down off the rooftop and out of this hotel. Some people are just sitting against the hallway wall, staring in disbelief. Others are howling in grief. It's complete insanity and Tommy knows they need to get out of here.

The stairwell is full of people heading down. The elevator isn't working anymore and that's okay for Tommy because he was planning on taking the stairs anyway. Maybe for the rest of his life, however long that will be. The memory of Mr. and Mrs. Chapman will follow him to his grave.

Let's just hope you're not buried in the Plantation Hotel.

"Come on," Jack calls out to him.

Dan and Skylar are not far behind them.

Tommy hasn't had time to make sense of anything. The bodies dropping all around them. The plane crashing into a building right in front of them. The earth shaking. Tommy's not even sure if Wilmington has ever had an earthquake before.

They reach the first floor only to find more confusion and chaos. A woman is behind the desk fielding questions from an unruly crowd. It's almost funny to see. Tommy accidentally steps on the chest of a guy with his mouth open wide and those dull eyes. Those fishlike eyes devoid of anything staring up at him. He fights a wave of nausea.

The building shakes again—another tremor. Maybe an aftershock. The sliding doors to the outside are shut. In the street, cars are trying to get through and horns are honking and people are yelling, cursing. It doesn't look any brighter or more hopeful out there.

Jack stops and looks around.

"This doesn't make sense," Tommy says.

"Yeah. People dropping dead. Earthquakes."

"Hopefully it's over."

Jack nods and wipes the sweat off his forehead. "Yeah, the worst is over. Has to be."

Tommy glances at Dan, who has his arm around Skylar. Tears still fill her eyes.

What are we supposed to do now?

He's about to turn and talk to Jack but a low tinging

sound begins in his ears. It's the kind that a television might make when you first turn it on, some kind of high-pitched sound you can barely make out.

Until it starts getting louder.

Tommy looks around and can see others noticing the same thing. The ringing quickly becomes more intense until people are wincing and holding their ears as the noise increases to a furious screech.

To Tommy it almost sounds like . . .

Is that a trumpet?

. . . one of those old-fashioned horns blown by military commanders. But louder than any sound he's ever heard. The blast sends Tommy and those around him to the ground. The building shakes again, and now Tommy wonders whether the incredible, awful noise is actually causing the shaking. The moment stretches out. He can *feel* the sound against his body. It's like a wave of terror rushing through and pressing him cowering to the floor.

Suddenly the trumpet blast—if that's what it was—stops. For a moment all is silent.

Tommy picks himself up and starts to head toward the outside parking lot when Jack yells at him. "Get away from the windows!"

Another aftershock shakes them and the windows. More screaming. More squealing of tires outside. Tommy's ears still hurt from that loud trumpet sound.

When the aftershock subsides, Tommy looks around. "Everybody okay?"

It's a stupid question because none of them are okay and probably never will be again but the key is just surviving this. Whatever *this* happens to be.

"My parents . . . and Lauren . . ."

They all look at Skylar. Her waterproof eyeliner doesn't seem waterproof anymore. Her wedding-day glow is long gone. Her hair is messed up and her dress is ripped and ruined. She's about to say something but Tommy gives her a hug to ward off more tears.

"I need to find Allie," Jack says.

"You don't even know where she is," Dan says. He's talking to Jack but looking at his new wife, still in Tommy's arms.

Tommy lets Skylar go and faces his two best friends. He doesn't have any ideas to offer.

"I'll figure it out," Jack says. "I'm not leaving her out there alone."

"Maybe we should just stay here," Skylar's weak voice says.

Tommy shakes his head. "We need to get outside. This building could collapse with another aftershock like that."

"My phone's dead," Jack says. "Anyone's phone work?"

Tommy's already checked his several times but grabs it to check again.

"Do you have my phone?" Skylar asks Dan. "Maybe she texted me."

Tommy suddenly remembers he texted Allison just after she left the reception. *Maybe she texted back.*

As Skylar's trembling hand tries to check the messages on

her phone, Tommy goes through his. Sure enough, he finds the last message Allison sent him. "She's at 45 North Street."

Jack gives him a surprised look. "How long ago did she send that?"

"Half hour ago. Let's get out of here."

Tommy starts to head out the front underneath the glass but Jack stops him. "Not under those windows. The side exit."

They are forced to stop again and cover their ears when another piercing sound cuts through them.

"What was that?" Jack asks.

Another trumpet blast? Tommy thinks but doesn't say. Ignoring Jack's warning, he rushes to the wall of glass windows and looks at the darkened sky. A sliver of silver lightning zigzags through the air, so bright it makes Tommy squint. It's not normal lightning. He can tell by the way it moves, by the way it just stays there in the sky, a bright line of brilliant calligraphy.

Thunder crashes. Tommy barely registers Jack yelling behind him—"Get away from the windows!"—and suddenly the front windows all explode. For a moment Tommy just stands there, dumbfounded and frightened. He's still mesmerized by the images in the sky, the marvelous streaks of lightning he keeps seeing.

So spooky and glorious . . .

Then someone pounds into him and pulls him away from the falling shards of the atrium. Glass rains down where he was just standing.

More screams and more shouts.

More sirens and more squeals.

More madness.

"Let's get out of here now," Jack yells, pulling at Tommy's coat.

He feels like he's in a drunken fog or some kind of frenzied nightmare. But Tommy runs. He follows Jack just like Skylar and Dan. They're running down the padded carpeting of the hallway toward a side exit. Away from more falling glass.

"Jack, slow down," Dan calls.

"I gotta get going," Jack says. He's like a man possessed with one mission on his mind: find Allison.

"Wait up," Tommy calls out. "Just hang on a second."

"We're going with you," Dan says.

"What are we going to do?" Skylar asks.

"We have to stay together." Even now Dan speaks with confidence.

"We gotta go," Jack replies. "Now."

Tommy looks at Skylar. He's never seen so much terror on someone's face. Especially a face as beautiful as hers.

He keeps breathing and keeps following Jack. There has to be some help outside. Somewhere. Somewhere in this bizarrely broken city.

14
ACTION

Some say the world will end in fire, some say in ice.

For a second Allison can't remember where she heard that. A song? No, not a song, a poem. It's a Robert Frost poem.

Or maybe it won't be fire or ice but earthquakes and sudden death.

The thought leaves her as she realizes the shaking has stopped and the deafening trumpet noise is gone too. The earthquake is over and there's a body pressed on top of her. It feels cold and heavy. For a few breathless moments Allison tries to push the body off her but has no luck. She's in the corner of the little church meeting room against the wall and somehow one of the dead people managed to topple *onto* her. Finally her body wiggles away as her eyes struggle to see. She hears a moan and for one horrifying moment thinks it belongs to the dead man.

"You guys? Beverly?"

A door opens and she can see a sliver of faint light coming from the hallway.

It's a man's voice but not the dead man's. "I'm here. I'm by the door. Can you see?"

"Yeah," Allison says. "Hold on."

She runs a hand over her legs, making sure nothing else is on her, then waves in the darkness.

"Excuse me—mister? Are you in here?"

"It's Jeff," the low voice says, adding a very loud curse.

"Are you hurt?" Beverly's voice.

"The table slammed against me. But I'm fine. Just trying to—move—here."

Allison's not sure what just happened. Her brain is telling her an earthquake, but she can't remember an earthquake ever happening in Wilmington. The world suddenly shaking isn't the scariest thing, however. It's the dead bodies in this room. And the dead body in the car outside.

Are there more?

Thoughts of her friends keep flashing in her mind. She tries to shut them off because she can't do a thing about them. She's not with them; nor is she with her family. She's stuck in a church she doesn't even attend, trying to figure this thing out with complete strangers.

"Here you go, honey," Beverly says as she takes her hand and leads her out of the room.

The three of them head down the hallway until they reach an atrium with a door leading outside.

"What the . . . ?" Jeff stares at them for a moment in a strange sort of silence. "I gotta check on my family," he finally says.

The world outside sounds angry and shaken. Allison only looks at the two of them, not knowing whether to go outside or stay in here.

"I think it's safer inside," Beverly says.

"I'm sorry; I just have to—"

And without even being able to say a word, not even a good-bye, Allison watches the man dart out the door and leave them behind. Sirens can be heard outside. Engines of some kind—cars or trucks or something. Voices yelling. The sounds certainly aren't inviting.

This guy—a pastor of some kind?—just left us.

"I'm not going back out there," Beverly says, making sure the bandage on her forehead is still there. "I think we should wait for help to come."

"You think anybody is going to come?"

"It's a church. Why'd you come here earlier?"

The woman has a good point.

"The power is out," Allison says, looking around for any sign of a phone. "You think it'll come back on?"

"I think we should try to find as many things as possible that can help us now. Especially since it's still light outside."

"Things like what?"

"Candles. Food. Anything that we might need later."

Beverly is about to wander down another hallway when Allison tugs her arm and stops her.

"What is it?"

"This is really happening, right?" Allison asks.

"I'm afraid so, honey. This isn't a dream you're going to wake up from."

"But what—what happened to those people? They just—they just died. Like that. Maybe like the guy driving the car that crashed into you."

"I'd like to blame our government, since I tend to blame everything that happens on them, but I don't think I can. I just think—I think we have to take care of ourselves and let the answers come whenever they decide to."

They're not the most encouraging words, but they are a call to action. Standing here and freaking out and wondering what's happening isn't going to help anybody, including themselves.

There is a slight rumble again.

"Come on—we might not have much time," Beverly says.

Allison wants to scream but she doesn't. She just keeps moving. Perhaps it will hold off the terror filling her heart.

15
FRENZIED

Things look worse outside the hotel. *Much* worse.

Jack seems to know where he's going, but Tommy can't tell for sure. Maybe he's only going around the cars that are stopped in the middle of the road. Maybe he's stepping around the bodies that are plopped right in the middle of the street or on the sidewalk like barricades. Everything he sees looks wrong and unreal. His mind wants to tell him this isn't happening, and he wants to scream himself awake, but Tommy knows better.

This is all real and there's nothing any of us can do.

Even if he did scream, he'd just be a voice in the crowd.

One of the many. Like the woman who walks by them muttering to herself in a jumbled and endless run-on sentence. Or the guy in the suit sitting against a building, weeping and staring at the ground. Or the couple holding hands as they rush down the street like there's some kind of rescue they're running toward.

Dan is holding on to Skylar. For a quick moment he glances at Tommy but doesn't say anything.

Tommy knows. Tommy can feel the terror in that look.

The dead bodies and the abandoned cars, some crushed and others simply stuck, aren't the only damage in front of them. The earthquake has left everything shaken and broken. Windows are blown out. Garbage cans overturned. A water line is flooding the center of a street. Smoke billows from a building. The smell of gas lingers in the air.

They pass the open door of a Mexican restaurant where the owner is yelling out curses at the sky. Tommy doesn't know Spanish very well but he can tell what the old guy is saying. Cursing is cursing in any language.

Jack stops at an intersection. For a second Tommy wonders what's wrong; then he sees it. The blonde ponytail. It belongs to a girl who must be seven or eight years old lying dead in the street.

"Oh man," Tommy says.

"This way," Jack tells them, heading down another sidewalk.

"What do you think did this? What killed all these people?"

Jack ignores Tommy's question as they walk. Dan and Skylar are moving slowly behind them, taking everything in with looks of dread and silent, open mouths.

"Why are we still alive?" Tommy continues. "What was that earthquake? And that lightning—I've never seen lightning like that before."

"I don't know, Tommy." Jack sounds confused, irritated, stressed. He stops for a minute as if to make sure they're heading the right way.

"Their eyes," Skylar says. "Did you see their eyes?"

I did thanks for mentioning it and oh yeah I saw your parents' eyes and I can't forget about them.

"Is this an alien invasion?" Dan asks.

Tommy looks at Dan to make sure, but he can tell Dan is serious just by his tone.

Jack looks sharply at him and shakes his head. "Yeah, Dan. I'm sure it's an alien invasion. Maybe Tom Cruise or Will Smith will come save us."

As they walk across a street, a man is pulling someone out of the back of an SUV that is pinned in place by cars. Tommy almost goes to help the man, but the stranger doesn't seem to want help.

"Come on," Jack says. "This way." He leads them through an alleyway littered with bricks. Tommy sees a No Trespassing sign painted on the side of one of the buildings flanking the alley. As they near the end of the narrow passageway, they see a cop and an elderly man pulling someone from the rubble of a building that must have collapsed. Jack keeps going, walking across another road.

When Tommy exits the alley and reaches the street, he's able to see the sky again. It has an eerie, muted yellow glow to it, one he's never seen before.

This is bad.

He's moving fast just like Jack but then he notices Skylar lagging behind.

"Skylar, you okay?"

She's almost in a trance. The sky must've freaked her out a bit too. "I think I know what's happening," she says.

"Huh?" Tommy says.

"I heard my parents talking about this for years."

"Talking about what?" Dan asks, out of breath as he wipes his forehead.

"The end of the world. Like it happens in the Bible."

Jack overhears and calls back, "Don't be ridiculous."

"It's not ridiculous," Skylar says. "The good people have been taken away and the bad are left here."

"No," Tommy says as he smells gasoline leaking from a wrecked car they pass. "There's got to be a scientific reason for everything that's happening."

"You're wrong," she says. "I'm telling you, this is straight out of the Bible."

Tommy shakes his head. *She's just being irrational.* "Look, you go to church, right?"

She looks at him and nods. "Yeah, so?"

"So you're not a bad person and you're still here, so it can't be just the bad people left here. Anyway, what you're saying is crazy. It's obviously not the biblical end of the world."

Skylar doesn't seem to like Tommy's answer. "Yes it is. I know it is."

Jack stops for a moment and curses. "Stop with the make-believe religious mumbo jumbo, okay? It's happened. It's done. We all survived. The world isn't ending."

Skylar breathes in, then swallows. She brushes back strands of her hair and looks at her friends.

"We need to find safety," she says in a calm voice. "If I'm right, this is gonna get *really* bad."

"If it's going to *get* really bad, then what do you call this?" Jack shouts back.

Skylar doesn't reply. There aren't words to sum this up. There are curses and profanities and screams, but that's about it. Mere words would seem too normal and kind compared to what's all around them.

A few moments later, Tommy feels something change. The temperature, the wind, the light around them . . . Something is different. Something is strange. Something is bad.

They are at an intersection where a cop is waving a crowd on. Where they're supposed to go, or what's supposed to happen once they move past, Tommy has no idea. There's a stalled bus in the middle of the road.

Wonder how many people are dead in that bus?

They're about ready to pass the bus when Tommy sees the look in the cop's eyes. He's not even trying to disguise it. The round, chubby face is a road sign for terror, his eyes seemingly blinking in warning.

"Hey, what's happening?" Tommy asks.

They move around the bus and now have a perfect view of the sky and the horizon between the buildings. What they're suddenly looking at, just like all the speechless spectators around them, is unlike anything Tommy has ever seen.

"Look at that," Jack calls out as the brilliant collage changes before them.

The yellow glow of the sky has turned into a menacing canvas of dark red. The clouds stand out and seem to be moving and alive. Not like pretty little powder puffs but like poisonous plumes.

Second by second, the sky grows darker.

As it does, Tommy grows more fearful.

For a second he's about to say something to Dan and Skylar, who are right behind them, but then the gunfire starts going off.

Wait—not gunfire. More like . . .

He sees something scattering in front of him. Spilling . . . no, blasting all around him.

Something explodes right on the street next to his feet. Tommy now reaches down and touches melting ice.

"What is that?" Dan asks. "Hail?"

Tommy shakes his head. "There's no way. Can't be."

It was the size of a basketball before it blew up. Maybe even bigger.

Another explosion of ice.

"It *is* hail," Tommy shouts.

Someone screams. Then the crowd starts to disperse in a flurry of noise and movement and images.

Something hits Tommy hard on the shoulder, then digs into his skull.

"Oh my—" Jack starts to say but then breaks off and screams for them to run.

The next few moments are like trying to evacuate from some kind of theme park that's suddenly gone out of control. The hailstorm is crazy. Tommy runs up next to the building as his legs and arms and head all get beaten and battered by hailstones the size of baseballs. Larger ones just miss him. A store entrance is closed so he keeps running down the street. Jack is in front of him and surely somewhere behind him are Dan and Skylar.

A woman is crying. *Is it Skylar?*

Tommy's right ear is nicked as if it just got shot. He's still running, searching, looking for somewhere or something or—

A car in front of them explodes with glass and metal as something out of a Superman movie crushes the vehicle.

That's a meteor not a piece of hail.

The immense thing would have killed somebody if it had landed in a different place.

"Come on!" Tommy keeps running, dropping his camera for a moment, then picking it up again and sprinting as he is pelted by another round of hail.

We gotta get off the street into one of these buildings, any of them.

Jack's got the same idea when he finally comes to a door that opens for all of them.

Who knows what they'll find inside.

16
HESITANCY

Allison stares out the window, thinking of an image that now haunts her.

A small, black-and-white booklet of twenty or thirty pages. Such a simple way to show how the world's going to end.

She can remember finding it that one day when she was just a kid.

Left in our mailbox from one of those people coming around. Somebody from a nearby church. Maybe one of those who knocked on our door not long ago.

It showed the dark clouds and the lightning.

And people cowering on the street corner in fear.

And people on their knees praying and crying out.

Angry figures straight out of the movie Gladiator *hovering in the heavens while sickly, angry-looking men slip through their shadows.*

Reading it back then didn't make sense to her. But even now, as an adult, the words don't seem logical or practical or reasonable in the least.

They're all about God's judgment and righteousness but nothing about his love and grace and hope.

Nothing but anger and wrath.

Nothing but condemnation.

This warning had only made Allison more resistant to whatever those people wanted her to know.

So many years ago and yet I can still see my hands trembling while I held the tract.

A voice snaps her out of her reverie. "It can't be happening. Not now. Not like this."

It's not the words that scare Allison but rather Beverly's tone. She doesn't sound surprised that they're watching some freak-show hailstorm outside producing massive ice balls coming down from the sky. Beverly just sounds surprised that it's happening today, as if she had it penciled on her calendar for next Friday.

"What do you mean?" Allison asks, looking away from the window and back into the darkened room.

"All this time I thought I was prepared."

"You've been preparing? For this?"

Beverly is still looking outside with a hypnotic fascination. "Unfortunately . . . yes."

"But I don't get what you're saying."

"I'm saying . . ." The older woman moves and faces Allison. "I'm saying I should be home. That's where I planned to be when the end came. We have a basement that has a shelter in it."

"Oh."

"Now, don't give me that."

"What?" Allison asks.

"One of them *oh*s like I'm some kinda crazy woman or something. I'm not. You see what's happening. Earthquakes. Trumpet sounds blasting from the sky. Hail the size of human heads. I knew that sooner or later the end was gonna come. I just expected to be home to help my family when it did."

"And I thought I was having a bad day," Allison says, then lets out a nervous laugh that feels good.

"Why are you here, anyway? You runnin' from something?"

"Yeah, maybe."

Allison thinks about finding that tract in their mailbox when she was just a young girl. She never showed her parents but hid it. Every now and then she'd pull it out and see the comic-book characters all terrified with no hope in sight. The words on the tract talked about wars and people disappearing and Israel and quoted lots of Bible verses too.

Why am I thinking about that?

"Wanna tell me?" Beverly asks.

"Boys."

That's enough of an answer. Beverly just nods and says, "Uh-huh." She pauses a moment. "You know, I'd normally say most things are the fault of men. But this here—I'm not sure."

"I need to get outside," Allison says.

"What? Didn't you see that sky? It turned the color of blood."

That's very comforting. Thank you for sharing.

"I don't think we're going anywhere anytime soon," Beverly continues.

Allison wants to put some jeans and flat shoes on. To wash the makeup off her face. To find herself closing her eyes under a showerhead and feeling the hot water against her face.

She wonders if the shower she took this morning was the last shower she'll ever take.

Stop it, Allie.

"So, your friends. . . . Tell me about them." Beverly is sitting on a cushioned bench in the foyer of the church.

Allison sighs and sits down next to her. "We're all college buddies. My best friend, Skylar, married a guy named Dan. They're so sweet together, so perfect."

It stings a bit saying their names. Allison knows they might be like some of the people she has seen, suddenly dropping dead for no reason.

"I was the maid of honor," Allison continues.

"And you escaped to a church. I'm assuming during the reception?"

She nods. "My boyfriend—Jack—he doesn't quite have the same romantic view of marriage that people like Skylar and Dan do. We've been dating for—for a long time."

"My husband was the same way. He didn't have a particularly fond view of marriage. Of course, I didn't know it until it was too late."

"Did he . . . Did you lose him?"

Beverly notices her serious tone. "Oh, yes, but not today. Not now. He left me."

"I'm sorry."

"Yeah. Me too. He went to bed my husband and then woke up someone else. Like a light switch was turned off. It took me years to realize there was no light switch there to begin with."

"That's awful."

"That's life," the woman tells her. "Maybe it's better that you know about your boyfriend's reluctance now before it's too late."

They hear something crash outside. Allison keeps breathing steadily but feels like she's at a higher altitude, like she can't quite catch her breath. "It sorta seems like we've gotten to the too-late stage already, you know?"

"We need to keep saying our prayers," Beverly says. "That's all we can do."

All we can do.

Maybe I can finally start to do it.

Maybe.

Suddenly another trumpet sound interrupts any thought she might have, either in her head or spoken out loud.

The sound is accompanied by more rumbling. It's not just the hail hitting the ground. It's everything around them. The ground and the church and the walls and everything.

Once again, the earthquake almost seems to be coming from the sound itself.

A piercing, deafening, haunting trumpet sound from heaven.

17
THE STRANGER IN THE DARK

The figures huddled together in the shadows could be alive or dead. Tommy's not exactly sure until he hears some muffled voices. Then whimpers, very low, as if noise will hurt and cause more pain. It's a bit scary and he leaves the strangers alone.

It takes him a few minutes to realize where they are. Once the skies started raining icy death balls, he and the others scampered like dogs with their tails tucked between their legs. The nearest opening—broken glass doors that they dashed through—led into a large, open space with tables shuffled around and books scattered on the floor.

When Tommy sees a cabinet of index cards, he finally understands.

Their shelter is the Wilmington Public Library.

Guess it takes the end of the world to get me to step foot in a library.

The humor in his head is good because if he loses it, he might lose his sanity, too.

Tommy is near the front when the trumpet blast rocks the building. Not a let's-rock-out-with-the-band sound but another explosion of noise that literally rocks and shakes the whole building. He grabs a bookshelf and feels the rattling while the sound seems to be piercing the center of his brain.

"What the—?"

He can't even hear his own words.

The lights inside the library go off and on, giving the room the feel of a futuristic disco. Tommy feels cold and heavy and really not so good. The way he used to feel when he did something bad and was about to have to face his parents. Or the way he feels at funerals. Awful with all this unexplained *stuff* deep inside him.

When the blaring finally stops, the people in the library are talking louder. More people are crying. More voices cursing and talking with question marks.

"Where's Skylar?"

Tommy looks and finds Dan at the entrance to the library. His new wife is nowhere in sight.

"Skylar!" Jack calls out.

They head into the dark pit of the library with Dan leading the way. The books tossed about look as disheveled as the bodies they've seen in the hotel and on the streets. Chairs are turned over. A decorative art piece is now dangling upside down. The farther they walk, the darker it gets.

She didn't just disappear.

But calling out for her doesn't get them anywhere. A whole bookshelf lies facedown on the floor. The lights still twitch on and off.

"Skylar? Where are you?"

Dan's voice sounds hoarse and weak. Silence reigns as the hallway opens up into more tall shelves of books. Dan heads down one aisle while Tommy takes another.

For some reason, Tommy expects someone to jump out of the shadows.

Maybe it's the dead bodies that are making me think this way.

He hears Dan's footsteps nearby, then can hear Jack calling out her name.

"Sky—"

The rest of the name is lost when the earth suddenly bounces back and forth like a yo-yo. Whoever's holding the string is yanking hard.

Tommy goes headfirst into a shelf of books as a dozen volumes topple over onto him. He feels the building swaying and the shelves moving and everything is black and violent.

Just as he begins to try to move forward Tommy feels something jam against his heel and he goes flying just like all the lifeless books around him that are never going to be read. He lands on his side and feels something thick and unmovable.

That better not be what I think—

But his eyes tell him the truth.

It's a body.

He jerks back and gets to his feet just as he hears someone to his side.

"He's dead," a female's monotone voice says. "He won't bite."

Whoever's talking isn't Skylar.

Tommy stands up and tries to compose himself in front of whoever is there. The lights are still flickering, so Tommy can barely make out the girl in front of him. He spots black eyes. For a second, he thinks he's seeing things, then figures out she's wearing heavy eyeliner. It contrasts well with her short, spiky white-blonde hair.

"Name's Sam," the teenager says.

The world's ending and I'm being rescued by a Goth girl.

"Uh, hi. I was kinda—"

Once again he's interrupted, this time by Skylar herself. He spots her racing through an aisle and then heading down another without even noticing them. She clearly is looking for someone or something.

"Skylar, stop," he yells as he starts to follow her.

He can hear shuffling behind him and realizes that Sam is following him.

"Is she wiggin' out?" the Goth girl asks.

Tommy wants to tell her that nobody is "wiggin' out" and please stop following him. But he's too focused on following Skylar. She's scanning the bookshelves—the ones that still have books on them—and obviously searching for something in particular.

This is crazy the world's ending and she's wanting to check out a book.

"What's going on?" he asks. He glances behind him, and the girl is still there, looking like a lost puppy with black eyes. "Skylar?"

"There's got to be a Bible in here," she says to Tommy as she glances at him for a second. "I'll prove to you what's going on."

He waits to see if she's joking, but Skylar is very serious. She's doing what she does best: taking control, trying to handle the situation.

No amount of anything's going to prove anything about what's happening.

"Two rows over," Sam says in that same unemotional tone. "Religion."

Skylar doesn't stop to ask who the girl giving the answer is or how she happens to know where to look. Tommy stares at her for a moment, thinking about asking himself, when he hears a triumphant cry coming from Skylar.

Tommy and Sam both walk over to find her standing next to a pile of overturned books, thumbing through a Bible.

No longer triumphant, now she looks confused. "It's not here. Where is it?"

Skylar is still in her wedding dress, still this vision of white in a shadowy place. Her makeup has started to run and her hair is flat but she seems to have forgotten about any of that. She's looking for answers and thinks a Bible is going to provide some.

Dan appears by her side and asks her what she's talking about.

"The Rapture. It's not in here."

A few hours ago Skylar and Dan were talking about their future and their honeymoon and all their wedding presents and all the love around them and now this. Now the world is shaking and Skylar's thumbing through a Bible and talking about the Rapture.

She finds something. "Here."

Dan doesn't say anything and looks nothing like the confident, happy guy Tommy saw earlier in the day.

"Hail." She looks at all of them to make sure they're paying attention. "Listen—'And there came hail and fire mixed with blood.'"

"That's not helping, Skylar," Tommy says.

She ignores Tommy and keeps reading silently. Then she closes the Bible and shakes her head.

"I don't get this. I shouldn't be here. I went to church. I did everything right."

Tommy wants to tell her that church has nothing to do with this, that the earth shaking has absolutely nothing to do with Sunday morning and singing some happy hymns. This is global warming maybe. Or perhaps some kind of terrorist attack, though that doesn't quite explain the earthquakes or the sky or really anything.

Aliens or God or Lysol spray cans so what? It doesn't matter who's responsible for the skies falling. That doesn't change anything.

"Let's not worry about trying to figure it all out right this very instant," Tommy tells her.

"The people—all those who just dropped in an instant—I always heard—the story always went that they would just vanish. Disappear. I never thought they'd be here. Or not they, I mean. Just their bodies."

Tommy stares at Skylar and doesn't know what to say.

She's gone crazy. Pure and simple.

"I know this is the Rapture. The end of days. Judgment Day. Armageddon."

"Those sound like a series of bad movies," Tommy says, trying to keep things light even though he's feeling absolutely opposite of that.

Dan urges Skylar to go back to the front of the library, where they're not so trapped in the shadows. He puts his arm around his bride to comfort her. "It's okay," he tells her. "We're going to be okay."

Tommy hears this but doesn't believe him. He peeks back and sees the Goth girl trailing him. There's nothing he can do. He can't exactly tell her to get lost. How can he turn anybody away in a world like this?

But he's not going to tell her or anybody that they're gonna be okay.

Nothing's going to be okay. Not today, and not tomorrow.

Maybe not ever again.

18 SNAPSHOTS

There must be something I can do.

This is all Skylar can think because this is all Skylar knows. But the comfort from Dan and the sanctuary of the library can't keep the fear from filling her. Reminding her of what's happening and what happened to her parents and what might happen to them any second now. . . .

I need to stay strong for her.

Dan keeps close to Skylar as they walk to the front of the library hoping to find someone with some answers. He tries to keep his body from shivering and tries to shake the awful terror filling his mind and his soul. . . .

We gotta get out of here and find Allison.

Jack is a caged beast, restless and furious at himself and everything else for letting Allison slip away. She left at maybe the worst time ever and all he can do now is try to find her and see if she's still alive. Try . . .

Keep moving keep breathing keep telling yourself you're alive and that's what matters.

And it does matter to Tommy that he's still alive. That his friends are alive. Except for Lauren, who seemed to somehow know this might happen. Lauren, who told him she was experiencing strange visions and nightmares a year ago. Lauren, who now is dead and whose words now haunt him. . . .

Stay with these people.

Sam doesn't want them to know how terrified she is and how desperately she needs to stay with other people. But she knows she can't be left here on her own. She saw the guy named Tommy with the kind eyes. She knows she should stay with him. She believes he can help her stay alive. . . .

Where are you?

Allison looks out the window and watches and wonders if she'll ever see Jack again. If she'll see any of them—Tommy, Skylar, Lauren, Dan. She thinks of her family and her friends and then back to Jack. There are words that still need to be said and may never get uttered. . . .

19
DROPPED OUT OF THE SKY

The sliding doors of the library are gone and glass covers the entryway floor. Tommy stands looking out on the street. The sky is dark and rain is falling to the ground. It feels colder outside even as he wipes the sweat off the back of his neck. He checks his iPhone for the hundredth time.

No connection and low battery. Soon I'm not even going to be able to turn it on.

Jack is pacing, needing to stay on the move, desperate to find Allison. "We gotta get to 45 North," he yells out.

The rain seems to hear him and responds by falling harder and louder.

"We're not going out there," Skylar shrieks.

She's becoming unraveled. Actually, they all are.

Tommy watches his friends, then sees Skylar is still holding the Bible in her hands.

This gives Tommy an idea. "Allison might be at the church on Camp Street."

Jack stops for a second and just glares at him. "She texted you 45 North."

"Yeah, but she goes to that church when she's upset. I bet she's pretty upset right now."

Jack stares in disbelief. "Since when does Allie go to church?"

"Tommy's right. Every time you guys get into a fight she ends up over there," Skylar answers without even looking at Jack.

"You have no idea what you're talking about," Jack says.

"I'm her best friend."

"I think it's a new thing for her," Tommy adds, trying to dissolve any sort of impending argument. The last thing they need to be doing is yelling and screaming at each other.

"We're going to 45 North," Jack says again as if he's the designated leader.

Tommy glances at Goth Girl, who's just standing there at attention, watching them with a slight look of uncertainty. He doesn't blame her.

"Look, the church is on the way, and closer," he says. "We can check it—"

"What are you talking about?" Skylar shouts. "We need to stay here, where it's safe."

The wind blows in the cool moisture from the pouring rain. It sounds like a tropical thunderstorm outside.

Jack nods and ignores Skylar's comment. "Fine. We'll hit the church on the way, but she's not going to be there."

Without waiting, Jack heads out of the building onto the drenched sidewalk. The blurry motion of rain swallows him.

Tommy's about to leave too when yet another loud noise stops him cold.

The zombie death trumpet sounds again.

Hearing it gives him goosebumps. It's not just loud; it sounds like it's coming from *everywhere*. The skies and the library sound system and the ground and even his own skin.

"We're not going. Absolutely not." Skylar looks like she's about ready to cry or pass out. She clutches the Bible like a toddler holding a stuffed animal.

Tommy looks at Dan, who's standing right next to her, unsure what to say or do. This isn't like Dan, who's usually in control of the situation and the leader of the pack.

He looks like a kid in a new school on his first day of classes.

"Dan, Tommy," Skylar says to them, "let's just stay."

"She's right, Tommy. It's safer here."

The bride always gets what she wants. Even if her dress is a little dirty and torn.

Tommy doesn't buy it. Allison is alone. Now Jack is alone too. He needs to go after them.

"Come on," he calls as he ventures into the rain.

Tommy can see Jack half a block ahead walking or half running. He follows as the rain soaks him down. Soon he is wiping water from his eyes, nose, and mouth. It's getting darker out here, and he's having to squint because of the drops of rain. For a second he turns but doesn't see the bride and the groom following him. He keeps going.

He gets to the intersection and sees Jack stopped on the street looking at something.

Is that a dead body?

But even in the dim light, Tommy knows it can't be human. It's much too large. As he steps closer, he can see the smooth, brown hair and realizes that it's a horse—one of those animals that would pull a carriage to give people tours of the city.

A very dead horse, unless it's decided to just go ahead and take a nap in the road.

"Jack?"

His friend looks over and wipes his wet hair back, then lets out a loud curse. "I think this thing was thrown over here. Look at its back, the way it's all disfigured like the bones all broke in two."

Tommy looks the other way. A dead horse is a dead horse. No need to get so close and start imagining all sorts of things.

"Are they coming?" Jack asks.

"I don't know."

Which probably means no. But then again who really knows.

Jack stands and curses again in frustration. "We have to find her."

"I know. I'm going with you."

"We have to get out of this place."

"This street?" Tommy asks.

"No, this city."

"You think it's better in other places?"

Jack looks scared. Surely they all do. Including Tommy.

"I just know that standing in a building waiting isn't going to get us anywhere, you know? I'm not waiting around like this horse."

The rain is dripping off the animal's unmoving, sleek side.

"I'm not going to just stand around waiting to be sucked up into the sky and then dropped back down onto the street. Uh-uh."

Jack keeps walking.

After another moment of looking at the horse in the middle of the street, Tommy follows.

20
IN GOOD TIMES AND BAD

I know before she tells me. Before she begins to weep. Before she begins to make excuses.

"I'm sorry, Allison," she says.

I know the explanation that's going to come. Mom and Dad just aren't making it. There are things. Complicated things. Difficult things. There are simply unexplainable things. Things that a church or a counselor or prayers or even their own daughter can't help.

"We just think it's best . . ."

I could recite this speech myself if I wanted.

"Your father and I still love each other. . . ."

Yeah, of course you do, of course 'cause that's what people in love do; they separate.

"This doesn't change how we feel about you. . . ."

But maybe it will impact how often we see you or how you feel about yourself or your world or your parents or your everything.

Yeah.

"I didn't want to cry. . . ."

I want to tell Mom maybe she should've thought about that before marrying a man who turned out not to be the one.

"Say something, Allie."

But I don't want to say anything because there's nothing to say. It happens all the time and now it's happening to me and there's nothing I can do.

The growing noise of voices in the church makes Allison move away from the bulletin board of faces she's staring at. They're pictures of men and women who work with the children at this church. All of them are smiling—couples, elderly folks, all looking into the camera and posing so the parents will recognize who they are. The photos made Allison think of her own parents for a few solitary moments.

She heads back to the sanctuary of the church, where more people have arrived. A man with a beard and disheveled long hair brushed back out of his face stands near the front of the church talking to everyone. She moves closer to hear what he's saying.

"—to just stay calm. That's all we have to do right now.

There are going to be more people coming; I know that. And for those of us who aren't hurt, we need to help the people coming in who are."

He has a calming voice even though he looks a bit rough with his hooded sweatshirt and grimy jeans.

"Where's everybody coming from?" the man asks the crowd of half a dozen people sitting or standing around the pews.

"We were downtown getting ready to go to our favorite restaurant when all hell broke loose," a gray-haired man says. He has an arm around a woman who's surely his wife.

At least they have each other, Allison thinks.

"Half the people around us just . . . they just died—just like that," the man continues.

Several people start talking at once, basically agreeing and trying to recount their own version.

The man with the beard nods and holds up his hand. "Look, I know you guys have questions, and I know—we'll figure this out and stay together and help everybody else."

He sees Allison and directs his full attention to her. "Are you okay, miss?"

"Yes," she says. "We were in the back—a few people just—it happened to them too—I was with a woman—"

"I'm here," Beverly says as she walks up behind her. "This is Pastor Shay."

Allison doesn't believe her at first but knows there's no reason for her to lie. She nods and looks at the man, who smiles at her.

"Are you by yourself?" he asks.

"Yes."

But only for now, hopefully.

"I think more are coming. Even if this isn't the kind of place they'd normally find themselves."

If this man really is a pastor, Allison wants to start asking him questions. *Real* questions. Honest ones. The kind he might not want to answer. The kind that are bubbling and spilling out inside of her.

The kind she's had for a very long time but just buried and let go.

For a few minutes, he tells them where things are in the church. There are rooms in the nursery area that he wants to set up as places where the sick and injured can be tended. They also need to start stockpiling food and supplies. He wants to know if anybody is willing to volunteer to get more from outside. Allison sits in a pew and hears the tapping of the storm outside the stained-glass windows.

Not sure I'm going to want to set foot back outside anytime soon.

She shivers, then glances down at her dress and remembers she's still wearing the bridesmaid gown. If this were a movie, it'd be a comedy, because certainly there's no way someone would make the end of the world occur with her still in this dress and high heels. Her skin feels rough as she rubs her arms to try to get some circulation going again.

"You want me to find you something to cover up with?" Beverly asks her.

"No, I'm fine. Really."

"Listen, everybody," the pastor says in a louder voice to get their attention. "Look, I don't know if you pray, but that's all we can do for the moment. I don't know what—well, look, we're supposed to pray in good times and bad, right? So that's all I can do. That's all I'll ask you to do. And communicate with me and with others. We have to help those who need it, so let us know."

Allison thinks for a moment about where Pastor Shay paused for a brief second. Not even a second but a millisecond.

"I don't know what—well, look . . ."

Was he going to say he didn't know what was happening?

Do you know what's happening, Pastor? And if so, are you going to tell us?

She glances again at the colorful windows in the church. She wonders exactly what's out there and what the night is going to hold.

She's afraid to really find out those answers.

21
STORM AND SILENCE

The rain doesn't merely fall. It batters the small group moving in the darkness. Jack has been leading them down this street, acting as if he knows where he's going. Tommy is close behind. Dan and Skylar did decide to follow them after all.

The sky is an angry dark gray and very few people can be seen on the sidewalks or road. Every now and then, they pass a car, some empty and some not. Tommy has stopped looking to see the difference.

There is a dip in the road where it starts to decline below an overpass. Perhaps they'll be able to dry off. His suit is stuck to him, his boxers giving him a nice wedgie that's starting to burn. As if it's not enough that the world is suddenly ending right in front of him.

None of them talk as they follow Jack. Occasionally Tommy looks behind and sees Dan and Skylar trying to keep up. He also spots Sam following them, a reality he didn't want but obviously must deal with now. Skylar looks like a sopping mess, with wet hair and running makeup. It's hard to picture the bride and groom as they appeared a few hours ago.

Jack stops once he's beneath the overpass and clear of the rain.

Tommy catches up to him and lets out a sigh. "Are we going the right way?"

"You know a better way to go?" Jack snaps back.

"No—I have no idea where we are."

Tommy takes the video camera from where it was hanging under his shoulder and coat.

"What are you going to do with that?" Jack asks.

"With what?"

"Why are you still filming?"

"Do you see what's happening around us?"

"So are you going to send it to *America's Funniest Home Videos*?"

Tommy can detect the anger inside of Jack. "I don't know."

"The rest of the country might be gone."

"We don't know that."

Jack lets out a curse and heads to the edge of the

overpass where the rain is falling before him in a blurry, wet wall of motion. Tommy leaves him alone. Soon Dan and Skylar are standing close by, shivering and huddling together. Sam stands next to Tommy.

"What are you doing?" he asks her.

"I'm going this way."

The girl certainly has nerve even though she's only a teen.

"I think it's safer back at the library," Tommy suggests.

"I don't."

Sam moves forward, closer to Jack, closer to the wet world waiting for them.

Tommy looks at the short figure with hair that's still spiked despite the rain. *I'm not taking care of her.*

This is what he tells himself. But he already knows he's going to have to.

Ten minutes later, they see a streak of fire on the street. It's a startling sight, this burning trail that looks like car parts scattered on the road. Nobody can be seen, just this fiery arrow that they have to walk around to continue down the road.

"What do you think happened here?" Dan asks.

"Whatever it is must've happened recently," Tommy says.

He wonders if it's too soon to be wary of strangers setting up traps. He's seen end-of-the-world movies. The zombie shows. When things like this happen, people start losing their minds. They start battling and killing one another. They fight each other over cans of beans. They aim guns at one another even though they've never fired one in their lives.

But it's not like they have anything on them to steal. And surely people haven't resorted to that kind of insanity just yet. The craziness is happening to them and around them. People haven't lost their minds.

Not yet.

The street begins to turn to the right, heading toward another bridge. Jack lets out a loud "Look at that!"

More flames are waving to them from the bridge in the distance. A long, sleek wing of a plane sticks out over the cement railing, the rest of the plane burning brightly.

They all stop and marvel at the sight. Judging by the wing, it's not a small plane but one of those big ones, like a 747 or something. Tommy can't believe the bridge is still intact.

"No wonder everybody is gone," Tommy says.

It must have happened very recently, possibly the last time somebody decided to take the world and dribble it around for a few moments.

Tommy thinks of all the dead bodies on the plane.

If the virus-death-thing didn't kill 'em then the crash certainly did.

He wonders if the plane is all there or if it is missing pieces. Perhaps half of the plane is on the other side of the city. Or maybe it's on some island where the survivors will be lost for a while and wondering what's going on.

But in this case you're not gonna want to make it back home because home isn't there anymore.

The sound of the rain falling is suddenly replaced by a strange sucking sound that makes Tommy's cold, wet skin prickle with bumps. A sound coming from everywhere once again. Like a massive water-flushing system of some kind. Or a monster Godzilla toddler coming out of nowhere with its massive sucking straw ready to slurp them all—

Tommy's flying.

Blown back in the air.

Ten, twenty, thirty yards.

He lands on the side of the road on some wet grass and dirt, his head planted a few inches in the mud, his eyes looking upward and seeing debris floating around him. Someone screams. Someone curses. The wind and the rain and everything suddenly . . . stop.

Just like that.

Silence.

What just happened?

Another massive trumpet shrieks in the sky and makes him wince and put his hands on his ears. *Where is that sound coming from?* He looks over and sees Jack getting back to his feet, staring around, looking and wondering.

Tommy doesn't know how many times this mighty trumpet has sounded. Four or five times?

It's like they're in a really nightmarish version of their own dystopian flick with the horns going off every time . . . what? Every time what happens?

Something supernatural and freaky occurs.

The rain has stopped and now the only sound he can hear is the crackling of fire from the crashed jetliner.

"This is unbelievable," he says.

He thinks of Allison again. Then of Lauren and Mr. and Mrs. Chapman.

We're never seeing Allie again ever. And you're an idiot because you let her go didn't you you moron?

Tommy shuts up the voices in his head as he stands and waits. Will there be more? More fireworks or storms or sucking noises? More earthquakes and trumpet sounds?

None come, thankfully.

22
BURIED AND FORGOTTEN

Cold in the covers. Empty and alone. Frustrated and unfulfilled.

I can feel my body and know the mistake I've made.

I want to be warm and full and free.

I want to be happy.

I see the light go off and hear the footsteps and know he's coming back to this place, to his bed, to his girl.

But all I want to do is run away and wash off the mistake I've made.

But I can't go back.

There's no way to ever go back.

For some reason Allison finds herself thinking of Mike. The first and last guy in high school she slept with. It wasn't love and it wasn't some kind of crazy infatuation. It was more of a curiosity about the actual act. It was more of her acting out to show the world and her parents and anybody else who might care that she wanted to do what she wanted to do. Yet in the end, nobody except the senior named Mike knew.

Him and God.

She didn't feel guilt at the time. So many girls she knew were doing it and not really even caring about doing it. That's why she tried it. But nothing about it made her feel better. Nothing about it made the questions inside go away.

Now, for some reason, thinking about it, she feels guilt and shame.

But why?

It's not like it was that big of a deal. Nothing happened. It just—it just happened and then she went her way. So did Mike.

The deed was done.

So why in the world is she thinking of that *now*, when there's so much else to think about?

She's in the kitchen of the church and can see her hands moving around taking food items and placing them in a box. She's not talking to anybody; she's simply in her own little world. Like everybody else. Whether they're being loud or quiet, everybody around her is in their own world.

Wondering what's happening.

Wondering where God might be.

And maybe wondering things like she's wondering.

Thinking about past mistakes that were buried and forgotten. Past misgivings that simply evaporated in the hot breath of the busy day.

There's no going back.

Allison knows this. There's no way to go back to the family she was once part of. To the girl she once believed herself to be. To the dreams she carried around in her heart. To the hopes she once harbored but never uttered out loud.

No going back.

She's tried. She's done good things and spent time giving and helping and loving and being a good girl.

So why now? Why this? Why here?

Like the confused teenage girl who left a boy and a bedroom with questions and confusion, Allison remains quiet.

Quiet and alone in a church full of so many others.

23
A LITTLE LOST GIRL

The darkness feels thick, not just because of the fog and the lack of streetlights but because of how completely it seems to cover everything. There's very little difference at times between Tommy opening and shutting his eyes. He can see the faint figure of Jack in front of him, moving slowly down the street. The shuffle of feet can be heard behind him.

"Are you lost?" he asks Jack since they can't see anything like street signs or even much of the surrounding buildings to provide guidance.

"We're almost there."

Jack sounds annoyed, distracted, still on a one-man

mission to find Allison. Tommy refuses to think about what might happen if she turns out—

No. She's out there. She's still there.

Even though it's cold, his back is damp with sweat. He's thirsty, too, though he's not about to ask Jack to find a local coffee shop. His legs keep moving, but his mind and his heart are still back in the hotel, still back in that elevator. A part of him thinks they always will be.

"It just got so cold."

He hears Mrs. Chapman saying this as if she's right around the corner.

Tommy still holds the video camera as if he's planning on filming some more. Who knows? Maybe there will be something worth filming. Maybe they'll get out of this. Maybe there are other places where this insanity isn't happening.

Suddenly everything just . . . turns down. Even the sound of their own footsteps seems to have been swallowed.

"You hear that?"

"No," Jack says.

"Exactly. It just got quiet."

Jack stops the group for a moment in the middle of the road. Tommy turns his head to look back at the rest of them just as a low booming sound blasts all around them. He feels it in his chest and can't help but duck a bit, expecting a building or a plane to be landing on his head. But there's no motion around them, no kind of fiery storm or anything like that.

Then the pulsing begins.

It's thick and deep and sounds like the biggest drum in the universe being struck over and over again. Tommy looks to see where it's coming from but it's just out there, up there, around them all. It's coming from the dark, and the darkness surrounds them.

The pulse starts to build and crescendo and Tommy begins to feel sick. Then it stops.

He breathes in for a second.

Then another trumpet sounds.

Another mysterious, blaring, booming trumpet.

Like they're in some kind of end-of-the-world comedy and each new moment of doom is signified by these ridiculous trumpet blasts that seem to cut through your skin.

"What was that sound?" Skylar shouts behind them.

Tommy wants to smart off and say something like, "Which insane sound are you talking about?" But he can't. The moment doesn't feel very funny. Nothing feels very funny, in fact.

Someone—something—rushes past in front of them. Jack is still just standing there, apparently trying to figure out what to do. The dark mass in the night blinks past them like some kind of glitch on a black computer screen or a ripple in the middle of the ocean at midnight.

Then another shadow sprints through the murkiness in front of them.

"Hey," Jack shouts.

He saw it too so I'm not losing my mind.

Are there others like them rushing to get out of the way? Or people waiting to attack them for whatever reason?

Tommy looks around and sees Dan and Skylar right behind him, their worry seeming to tremble on their faces. Skylar's eyes look huge, full of the unknown. Dan's presence doesn't really seem to be providing much comfort.

It feels cold, much colder now.

"It just got so cold."

Tommy wants to start running down the road.

His heart races and his mind is splintered in ten million pieces all rolling around like tiny marbles down a hill.

A scream—no, several screams.

The pulsing sound—louder—thicker—closer—

The gray-black fog shakes and moves like there are more people or more monsters closer, sinking in, sneaking nearer.

No no no run away.

A clapping sound on the pavement. More howls.

Then Tommy sees something coming toward them—a large, sickly silhouette.

It's a horse. This one is alive, however. A horse pulling a carriage with a dead driver still holding the reins.

The tour guide of death passes by them and Tommy only scans the area wondering if something else is coming. Jack curses while Skylar looks down and shuts her eyes.

"What are you doing?" Tommy asks her, but it's obvious. More obvious than anything else going on around them. "Praying isn't going to help us."

Tommy sees a white face like a ghost staring at him. It's

Sam, the Goth girl, just looking at him as if she wonders what's next and what to do.

"We gotta go," Tommy says.

Jack is still cursing, which doesn't help the situation one bit. Jack screaming profanities and Skylar squeezing prayers and all of them stuck in this shadowy road.

We gotta get out of here before something else comes.

Another sound starts and Jack heads toward it.

It's a church bell in the distance. This one isn't from the skies. This sound actually seems normal, if that word can apply to anything right now.

"Come on," Jack says. "We gotta keep moving."

"Hold up, guys," Dan shouts.

Tommy turns and sees Dan still consoling Skylar.

"It's okay," Dan says. "I'm not going to let anything happen to you."

It looks like Skylar is shaking. This in itself is terrifying. The unshakable Skylar, the one normally so confident and in charge.

She looks like a little lost girl who's looking for her parents.

Skylar clutches Dan's hand. "Don't let go of me."

"I won't."

The bride and the groom, remaining together until the very end.

A thumping sound starts, then seems to be heading their way.

The air around them begins to move and change.

For some reason, perhaps because there's no other thing

to do, Tommy lifts the camera toward the sound and starts filming.

"There's something out there," Tommy starts to say.

The blur wraps itself around them.

A high-pitched buzzing sound that pierces his ears seems to coil around their heads and throats but still Tommy can't see anything. Not yet. Not just yet.

The air shifts and he can feel it—whatever *it* happens to be—moving. Shifting. Rushing.

What's happening?

He still holds the camera.

Something buzzes by his head. It's behind him, then at his side, then . . .

A figure, massive and beastlike, right in front of them.

Skylar screams. It's so dark, so foggy, so hard to see.

Tommy looks at Dan and Skylar but can only see Dan. He hears Dan now, howling like someone's peeling his skin off.

Skylar is not there. She's not on the street and not by Dan's side.

"She-was-there-and-then-she-was-just-gone," Dan screams in one giant, long, single word.

Jack is suddenly by their side, out of breath like he was running back toward them. "What was it?"

"I was holding her hand. She's not there. She's not there. I didn't let go."

Dan is out of his mind like some kind of crazy man.

This isn't happening. "What are you talking about?"

Tommy asks, looking around, knowing Skylar has to be around somewhere.

Nothing just *took* her.

No way.

"Did you really see . . . ?" He doesn't even want to finish his comment.

No.

Dan and Jack start screaming out Skylar's name while they all look around the street. The buildings on either side. The broken windows, the fallen debris, the empty cars, the alleyway leading to nowhere.

Tommy shouts her name too but he's out of breath, out of sorts. His head hurts and his eyesight feels blurry.

He then hears a sound. Another sound. An awful, hideous sound.

God make them stop make these sounds stop.

It's a woman's voice. It's Skylar.

Screaming.

Down the street somewhere.

Jack, Dan, and Tommy all run to her.

24
BLACK AND WHITE

For a moment or a lifetime—Skylar isn't sure—she knows she's no longer the person she once was, the girl who became a woman who turned into a bride today. She opens her eyes and sees the vastness of everything, all while the light and the dark do battle over her.

She hangs in the balance, drifting, falling.

The light is bright but she continues to fall into the deep well of darkness.

She's somehow not in pain in this place, even while being tossed and turned around. But she's alone. She's alone and empty and knows there's more. So much more.

The moment lasts an eternity as she is tugged back and forth, pulled and pushed and clawed and scraped.

The luminance above her quivers and she feels a rumbling as if the earth is trembling like before.

Then Skylar drifts off until she opens her eyes again to find herself sprawled over the sidewalk.

Dan and Tommy and Jack are running toward her. In the background, she can hear the bells of a church ringing.

I'm back.

"Sky, are you okay?"

She's dizzy and weak and can barely lift herself up.

"What happened? I heard you scream!"

She tries to answer but feels the darkness seeping back in. Then she feels someone's arms scooping her up and once again she's flying.

She pictures her parents. Together. Inseparable. Smiling. Arm in arm. Laughing.

It's the way it's always been, the way she's always seen them, the way she wanted it to be for her and her husband.

One day I'll have that.

It's not picture-perfect and she knows there have been struggles and difficulties. Some of them her parents shared, while others she knows they kept to themselves. She's old enough to understand. Or at least try to understand.

I want that kind of friendship.

They often said that it was God who kept them together, but Skylar has never believed it. It's the two of them making a daily choice, right? It's the two of them being patient and loving and forgiving and living.

Living together . . . and now dying together.

She doesn't understand what's happening and doesn't know what's going on and she still can't face the fact that her parents are gone. Truly gone.

She hears her mother again.

"God has watched over this marriage and this family."

So where are You now? Where are You, God? Did You decide to abandon every person who didn't give themselves over to You completely?

Skylar has her eyes closed but can hear the church bells growing closer.

The church will take them in, but then what?

It's only a building made of bricks and wood. A structure that can easily be ripped apart like the rest of the world around them.

Will we find safety inside?

Safety from the darkness hovering just below the light?

The darkness that tried to tug her away and keep her deep inside.

Just as they're about to enter the church, the screams begin.

Horrible screams coming from the area they just left.

That could have been me.

Skylar is still being carried by Dan. She opens her eyes and sees him. He looks shocked, desperate, tired.

For a moment, he looks at her and she sees him try to get rid of all those emotions.

He smiles. "We're almost there."

Her eyes start to drift back toward the darkness again.

25
TRAPPED

The light glimmers like some kind of solitary lighthouse on the edge of an island under a blanket of thick fog. They rush toward it, hoping and praying the light is a good sign. Everything else around them—everything that Tommy can see—is just darkness. Desolate and gloomy. Forgotten. Abandoned.

But hope lies ahead. So all of them anxiously expect.

As they draw closer, the building's outlines come into dim view. It's a church.

They arrive and try to open the front doors but they're locked.

Who locks the doors of a church?

Tommy can't help letting out a curse. They've escaped from all this insanity behind them only to get here and find locked doors. Really?

Jack starts pounding on them. "Let us in! We need help! Help!"

He's almost losing his voice from screaming so loud.

There's a very long, very quiet moment where nothing happens. Nothing except Tommy's heart crumbling and his blood beginning to boil. Until the sound of a latch unlocking can be heard, then the two wooden doors opening.

"Get in," a man tells them. "Come on, hurry."

Tommy waits to be the last one inside. He peeks up at the night sky and can see hundreds, maybe thousands, of what look like dark streaks descending from the heavens.

What are those marks?

They're like claw marks on the wall of a prison. They sicken his stomach.

He rushes inside and hears the doors closed and locked behind him.

The man who welcomed them in is the same one who makes sure the doors are locked. He's got long hair and a thick beard along with dark bags and wrinkles under his eyes. He's wearing a sweatshirt and jeans. He's probably like them—some guy running in the darkness who saw the church and sought refuge.

"Is she all right?" the man asks.

Dan is holding Skylar up. "I don't know."

They head from the entryway into the main area of the

church. Dim lights show strangers huddled in the shadows. There are couples embracing. Lone figures sitting in silence. Groups comforting those weeping.

This might be a place of sanctuary, but it looks more like a prison.

As Jack helps Skylar sit on a pew, Dan looks around and cries out for assistance.

"Get her some help," he screams, his voice on the verge of sobbing. "Please . . . please, please, somebody help her."

The man who helped them in is standing over Skylar. Tommy watches as the man examines her. The front of the beautiful white dress she was married in is now discolored and contains ashy burn marks all over it. Her shoulders are bruised and dirty and the sides and back of her dress are torn.

Then Tommy sees what the others must have already noticed. Two stab wounds on her back that are bleeding slightly.

The short, blonde-haired Goth girl pops out of nowhere to give Skylar her Bible. "You dropped this," Sam says.

As she hands it to Skylar, the Bible starts to fall apart. Pieces crumble away like the ashes of a fire that's been out for a long time.

"It's burned," Sam says, visibly shocked.

"The words," Skylar says, her voice weak and soft. "They're all gone."

Dan is still looking around the church, seeing if anybody can help, standing guard at Skylar's side while talking to the others. "What did that to her?" he asks the long-haired man. "Do you know what's happening?"

"Just make sure the doors remain locked," the man tells all of them.

"Are we safe here?" Tommy asks.

He's having his doubts now that he can see everybody. The terror on their faces is very real. All he can see are adults trapped inside this dim space. It doesn't matter if it's a bomb shelter or a church building. It's the same empty, ensnared place they've all somehow decided to hide out in.

The man shakes his head, looking panicked. "I don't know. I think . . . I think we're okay. Let's take care of your friend. Hey, Brad, Donny—can you guys take her to the preschool room with the other injured? Find Rachel."

Dan doesn't leave Skylar's side and doesn't let her hand go. Two more strangers, Brad and Donny apparently, come and help Dan with Skylar.

"I'm Pastor Shay," the man tells them as he shakes Tommy's hand.

"I'm Tommy. That's Jack. She's Skylar; Dan's next to her." For a minute he forgets Goth Girl's name. "Oh, yeah, and Sam."

The man doesn't look like a pastor, but then again, this doesn't look like a church. The city doesn't look like itself. Even the sky seems to be a stranger.

Nothing is normal. Not one thing.

"Skylar and Dan—it was their wedding day," Tommy tells the pastor.

"Some day to get married."

The pastor sounds cynical and bleak.

"Look, I'll make sure she's okay," Pastor Shay tells Tommy. "You guys stay here. Get comfortable. We might be here awhile."

The sigh Tommy lets out might be a little louder than usual. He doesn't care. He leans over and puts his hands on a pew and then he shuts his eyes.

He doesn't like being here. Trapped. Shut out. In a place that's no different than any other place.

He hears sobs. They make him a bit sick.

Nothing makes sense. He's not even sure how to *begin* to make sense of everything. But this isn't the place to do it. This is only going to confuse things.

A large cloth banner adorns the wall nearby. Tommy reads it.

> But as for me and my household, we will serve the LORD.
>
> JOSHUA 24:15

Jack is searching the room for Allison, calling her name. Tommy feels numb, knowing she's not here, wondering if she was ever in this church to begin with.

Me and my household.

Yeah, sure, Tommy thinks.

Maybe she never made it here. Or she left and got caught up in the madness outside.

He rubs his eyes.

"Jack," a familiar voice calls out behind him. "Tommy."

Tommy looks back up at the banner.

It can't be.

He turns and sees Allison.

Thank God she's still alive.

He suddenly feels a bit lighter, a bit brighter.

26
DEEP WOUNDS

Nobody noticed when she left the church sanctuary to walk down the dimly lit hall and go into a bathroom to have a nice crying session. But Allison couldn't help it. As people continued to come into the church—wounded, shell-shocked, holding each other—Allison waited and wondered if her friends might show up. But minute by minute, she feared the worst.

They're gone just like so many others.

She couldn't help thinking of her parents and the rest of her family. So far away, so unreachable . . . no way to know if they're alive. Just like Jack and Skylar and Dan and Tommy and Lauren.

She felt angry at herself, knowing she shouldn't have

left the wedding. Then she felt anger at Jack for letting her leave. But that just made her more angry at herself for even having emotions like this.

The tears lasted ten minutes, and then she began to walk back to the sanctuary.

That's when she saw them.

The boys, as she calls them, standing in the midst of the strangers in the shadows.

Allison calls out to them, and they turn to her. She embraces Jack and finds her eyes welling up again, but this time with tears of joy and surprise. She holds on to him and doesn't want to let him go. Jack crushes her with his hug, then kisses her forehead. She finds herself sobbing momentarily out of pure relief, her body shaking uncontrollably.

"You came looking for me," her voice barely manages to get out.

"Sorry it took me so long."

She finally regains control of her emotions and manages to look at Jack. He looks like all the rest—tired and messy and scared.

No, that's not right. Jack isn't scared. Staggered, maybe, and sickened, but not scared.

"I was trying to call. . . . Everything was dead. . . . How did you guys know I was here?"

Jack glances over her shoulder, then back at her. "Tommy."

She turns around and sees Tommy, then goes over to hug him as well.

"I didn't think I'd see you guys again," she says.

"We weren't sure we'd see you," Tommy tells her.

She looks around them for a minute and finally realizes they're alone.

"Where's Skylar and Dan? What about Lauren? Are they hurt?"

Tommy looks angry. "Skylar is being helped by a woman here. She was attacked out there. Dan's with her."

Attacked? By what?

Add the question to the never-ending list.

"Lauren's dead," Jack tells her without any emotion or subtlety. "They're all dead back there at the hotel."

It's too much to hear.

Lauren can't be dead. The others—all of the others at the wedding—

Allison's body starts to shake and the tears come once again. She's a mess but she can't help it.

Jack moves over to hold her. "We're going to be okay," he tells her. "All right?"

But she doesn't believe his words. She knows he's just trying to comfort her, but she finds no comfort in his declaration. She doesn't know what they're going to do.

Maybe Lauren and the others are the lucky ones.

Maybe they were spared the nightmare that's unfolding right here and now.

The pain is everywhere. It feels like a low hum, like a burner that's been left on and forgotten about but then you touch it and scorch your skin. Skylar hurts all over and can no longer even try to fight it. She's weak and knows she's close to slipping into unconsciousness. But Dan's next to her and they've finally reached where they were headed.

Skylar rests on a cot in a room that looks like it used to be for preschoolers at the church. Colorful rainbows and clouds and letters and Bible pictures adorn the walls. The tables and chairs have been moved and replaced by mattresses that a couple of people lie on. Light comes from a few lanterns, one being held by an African American woman who also carries a friendly smile with her.

"I'm Rachel," the thirtysomething woman says. "I'm a nurse. Let me take a look at you."

"What is this place?" Dan asks.

"It used to be a classroom. We've made it a temporary triage center. We got some medical supplies from a few places."

Skylar screams out in pain.

"I'm sorry," Nurse Rachel says. "Your shoulders—they're both dislocated. How'd this happen?"

Skylar swallows but her mouth is so dry. "I started to—there was this thing that came out of nowhere—attacked us—it grabbed me. . . ." Her voice is hoarse.

The nurse grabs a bottle of water on the shelf nearby and opens it. "Here, take a sip. That's right. Just a little."

The water tastes good. It spills down the sides of her mouth but Skylar doesn't care.

"This blood—where is this from?" Rachel asks.

"My side—I got stabbed with something."

"With what?"

"We don't know," Dan answers. "Some kind of thing out there."

The nurse doesn't react but just keeps checking Skylar over. Finally she looks up. "I need to reset her shoulders."

Dan seems nervous.

"This is going to hurt a little," Rachel says.

Skylar nods. "It's okay."

Dan comes to her side and holds her hand for a moment. "You're going to be fine, okay, Sky? Okay?"

She feels so tired and so wrapped in pain.

"Do you remember the first time we met each other?" Dan says quickly. "I remember when you walked into Jack's party. My jaw literally dropped. I'd never seen anyone so beautiful in my life. And now . . . now look at this."

He shows off his wedding ring while the nurse gently feels around Skylar's shoulders.

"On their wedding day, most brides hope that there's no rain or the band doesn't show up late," Skylar says in a weak voice. Then she chuckles and coughs. "I'm just hoping the world doesn't end."

"Well, if it makes any difference, the wedding was perfect all the way up to the end-of-the-world part."

She knows he's trying and she smiles at her husband.

"I love you, Mrs. Wilson," he says.

"I have to lift the arm to reset it," the nurse says. "Take a deep breath."

No, please . . .

She turns her head toward Dan and focuses on his handsome face, the smile she fell in love with, the eyes she never wants to let go.

"Mrs. Wilson," she repeats.

"Ready?" Rachel asks.

"I love you, too, Mr. Wilson."

The nurse lifts Skylar's arm and a waterfall of agony rushes over her. Skylar sees everything suddenly become bright. The burst of suffering is immense, unlike anything she's experienced, even unlike the attack itself. But then it's over and her shoulder has somehow found its way back into its socket. She unclenches her teeth, letting out a muffled gasp, her stomach all knotted up and tight.

"Good," the nurse says. "Now the left side."

"Maybe we should just give her a moment."

"No," Skylar says. "Just do it."

She can barely keep her eyes open. The pain claws and covers and she can barely suck in any oxygen since she's tightening every muscle in her body.

Just get it over with do it do anything just make the pain go away.

"Hey, remember when we drove to get our marriage license and the office was above that crazy deli?" Dan asks her, making sure she can see his face. "We waited to get a copy while staring at pigs' feet."

The memory makes her smile. "I remember driving back through the rain eating those Black Forest ham sandwiches. Best sandwich I've ever had in my life."

The nurse lifts her other arm and she grimaces. She feels woozy and everything begins fading to black. The pain pounds her but the shoulder pops back in and her arm is helped down again.

"Good job," the nurse tells her.

She can feel the sweat on her forehead and her back. The pain seems to go from side to side, first one shoulder where the puncture wounds are, then the other, then back again. Her back is sore, her legs numb. Her eyes close for a moment before opening again.

"We need to get that dress off her," Nurse Rachel says. "Dan, can you grab the sheet off the mattress over there and provide a little cover so I can help her change? I need to look at those wounds."

Taking the dress off is an ordeal that lasts fifteen minutes. Skylar can't move her arms much at all.

"This probably hurts more than resetting your shoulders," Rachel tells her.

With the bloody dress off, Skylar painfully stands while the nurse examines her wounds, cleaning them up and putting bandages over them. Soon Skylar is putting on some loose clothing that belongs to someone else. Then she lies back down on the cot. It feels good to close her eyes and just breathe slowly, in and out, in and out.

She feels the gentle kiss from Dan on her cheek.

Then she hears something ominous from the nurse. "I've never seen a wound like that."

Skylar thinks back to everything that's happened since her wedding.

I've never seen anything like any of this, ever.

27
HELL ON EARTH

The sound of the piano in the darkness feels strange and surreal to Tommy. He's looking for Skylar and Dan and has wandered down a hallway full of unoccupied and dark rooms. This church is bigger than he thought. Finally he comes to an open door and hears the music coming from the lighted room beyond.

It's an Elton John song.

The lantern propped up on the console piano in the corner of the room shows the outline of the pastor playing the song. He's quite good, Tommy realizes. He listens, then thinks he might be intruding, so he knocks loud enough to be heard.

"Oh, hey," Pastor Shay says. "Come on in."

Tommy walks into the room. It's full of chairs. It must be the place where the choir rehearses.

"I used to want to be a musician," the pastor says, looking down at the keys of the piano. "A rock star. Always loved music growing up and learned to play piano and guitar."

"That was pretty good."

"Yeah. But not good enough. I led worship for a church for a while, got into ministry that way. But I didn't want to be another Billy Graham. I was more looking to be Bono."

Tommy looks at the cross hanging on the wall nearby. "Do you have any clue what's happening out there?"

"A clue? Yes. It's the Rapture," the pastor says. "It's right out of the New Testament."

"Come on. The thing where Jesus teleports the good people—"

"The *believers*."

"—to heaven so all of us heathens—"

"The nonbelievers."

"—can live through a hell on earth?"

The pastor only nods his head.

"But no one got teleported. They all just died."

"You could say their souls got teleported, I suppose," Pastor Shay says. "I'll admit I didn't expect it to go down exactly like this. But there's no doubt about what's happening. We are all presented with the same evidence. I guess it's what conclusion we want to draw from it that ultimately matters."

"I don't draw anything from it." Even Tommy is a bit surprised by the anger in his tone. But it's the truth. The world is falling apart and no amount of Sunday school stories will change that.

Pastor Shay looks at Tommy for a long moment. "So what do you think attacked your friend?"

"Aliens, maybe. I don't know. I can't explain any of it."

"I guess we'll find out soon enough."

The pastor's voice is weary and reeks of defeat. Everything about this man strikes Tommy as strange, but that just fits with everything else going on.

There might be more for Tommy to say, more that he should manage to come up with even though he still has no clue what to think, but his might-have-beens are interrupted by the sounds of the church bell ringing.

"There must be more survivors arriving," the pastor says. "Let's go see who they are."

They enter the church sanctuary to find the room full of crackling fear. Everybody is standing up, a few people near the doors while most of the others are gathered near the front of the room. The faces appear relieved to see Pastor Shay.

"Who came in?"

"A small group," one of the men tells him. "Five people. Three are over there. Two of them went in back to the triage."

"What's wrong?" the pastor asks.

"One of them is pregnant."

A scream comes from the hallway.

Jack and Allison appear next to Tommy. "Let's go see if we can help," Allison suggests.

Tommy follows her and Jack down the hall. The screams get louder as they near the classroom that's now a designated area for the sick and wounded. He wonders how Skylar is doing and whether Dan is still by her side.

Soon they stand in a room full of confusion and chaos. As Tommy watches, he feels almost like he's floating, observing from somewhere outside his normal point of view as if he's hovering over himself and everybody else like some kind of surreal ghost.

A woman is writhing on a cot like some possessed figure, holding her protruding stomach.

Dim lights surround her while strangers stand not knowing what to do.

The nurse remains by the woman's side, getting things ready, putting a blanket over her, covering the ground with sheets, looking for other things.

Tommy doesn't see Skylar and Dan. Maybe they were moved somewhere.

"Here—you—wet these towels for me."

The nurse is talking to him. Tommy doesn't ask anything but rather rushes out of the room carrying the stack of towels. It takes him a moment to find the bathroom, but he finally does and wets down all the linens. Figures are behind him, strangers rushing down the hall, more standing in the triage area where the screams are coming from.

She sounds like she's dying.

He gives the drenched towels to the nurse. The woman on the cot is screaming and crying, her body moving everywhere. A man—her husband?—is trying to calm her down but isn't doing any good. The nurse blocks Tommy's view, but he can still hear all the violence and agony happening right in front of him.

"The baby's coming," the nurse says. "I can see the head."

Tommy stays near the back of the room, his head still feeling a little fuzzy. He's not supposed to be here, witnessing this event, being part of such an intimate thing. Yet he refuses to run away. He wants to be there in case they need him to do something. Anything.

The screams bounce off the walls. They're so loud and so close.

"You're doing good; come on," the nurse tells the woman.

They have hardly anything to help the woman in labor. No epidural. No pain medication. No anything. Just wet towels.

More crying, hollering, groaning, pushing.

Tommy feels like he's going to pass out. Jack has already left the room.

He can't breathe while he stands listening, wondering if the woman's going to make it, waiting to see if the baby is okay.

Those few brief moments feel like an eternity to Tommy.

What do they feel like to the mommy-to-be?

The nurse remains active, moving and bending over and grabbing tools on the table next to her. Tommy can't see what she's doing until suddenly she's holding something in her arms.

"It's a boy," the nurse says.

But there are no sounds of faint cries or tiny coughing. No sort of motion in the nurse's arms.

Where's the wailing that always happens with newborns?

Something is happening here, something awful, something Tommy doesn't want to see anymore. But the doorway is blocked. And Allison is standing right in front of him. He has to remain by her side and stay strong.

"Can I hold him?" the mother asks in a weak voice.

The nurse has her back to him, but Tommy knows something is wrong.

There's no sound a baby is supposed to be crying where are the cries now there needs to be some wailing going on.

"Please . . ."

There's an audible gasp from someone. The mother is sitting up and crying as she holds her baby.

"Why isn't he crying? I don't hear any crying!"

Allison turns around with tears in her eyes. Tommy wants to say something to her but instead she just buries herself in his arms and weeps.

"What is wrong with my baby boy?"

The screams of the mother are something that Tommy knows he'll never forget.

If he lives to be a hundred years old, he knows he'll be able to hear the anguished, tormented cries of this new mother holding her dead child in her arms.

Tommy holds Allison, knowing nothing is right anymore. Knowing there is no God because God wouldn't allow this. Not this. Not now.

28 UGLY

"Is she okay?"

The older woman who introduced herself as Beverly is asking about Allison. Tommy looks over to see Jack holding Allison in the pew. The muted light and low murmurs make everything feel more ominous and creepy. If they could just get out of this place with all of its religious mumbo jumbo and strange heavenly feelings, their outlook might improve. But for now, the place feels like a divine prison.

"She'll be okay," Tommy says.

It's been half an hour since Tommy witnessed the birth of the mother's dead baby. Now he doesn't know what to think or say. Allison is still weeping somewhat uncontrollably while Jack holds her and tries to make her feel better. Dan and Skylar are still somewhere in the back of the church, hopefully sleeping or at least chilling out.

"They keep coming in here," Beverly says.

"Yeah. While I want to get out of here."

Every now and then he checks his phone. It's dead and it's been dead for a while, but he checks it just in case. A few people have still been trying to make calls or connect with someone on their phones. Nobody's said they've gotten through, however.

Maybe there's nobody out there to get through to.

Pastor Shay steps into the sanctuary looking tired and sweaty. "Hey, Tommy. Can I talk with you?"

He wants to tell the pastor no, he doesn't want to talk. Surely the pastor is going to ask him to do something he doesn't want to do. And he'll probably do it because that's what Tommy does. He's the nice guy. He's the guy who isn't attached to anybody and he's doing what anybody else asks and those guys always—*always*—get killed off first in horror movies. They never make it to the end. Who cares if they live or die anyway? It's usually the girl with the guy at her side who makes it to the end.

"I need you to help me downstairs in the basement," the pastor tells him.

There's a basement? Wonderful.

Of course he nods. Of course he's going to follow the pastor down into the basement. At this point what else is there for him to do?

Well, maybe you can pray and ask . . . Oh, wait, you don't do that.

Pastor Shay's eyes are grim as they scan the pews of the church. He doesn't appear to even want to reach out and help anybody. Instead he looks pessimistic and frightened. "Come on then," he tells Tommy.

A hallway leads to a door that opens on a set of concrete steps. This would be where the pastor turns out to be a serial killer in the horror movie that Tommy wouldn't survive.

He's leading Tommy to a dark passageway lit only by the shaking glow of his lantern.

Soon they open a door and enter a room that looks like storage. There's a door at the back of the room. Tommy half expects to see something freaky like a mannequin that maybe looks like the pastor coming to life and talking to him.

"Half this basement is unfinished," Shay tells him as he opens the door and leads Tommy into a cold, massive room.

The first thing Tommy notices is that the floor is dirt. It's soft, the air musty. Metal pillars are placed in strategic positions around the open area. For some reason, Tommy thinks of his favorite television show when the main character was burying money in the crawl space. Yet this is much larger than a simple crawl space. There's no crawling necessary down here.

"We always imagined finishing this space off eventually," Pastor Shay says, walking toward the side wall of the room. "Guess there's really no point now, huh?"

Tommy doesn't reply. He spots a shovel and then gets why he's here. Next to a shovel, he spots a couple more. Then he sees the pile of dirt close by.

They're graves. Somebody's dug fresh graves down here.

"I didn't want a bunch of dead bodies upstairs freaking people out," Shay tells him. "We've been burying bodies all night."

Tommy wants to throw up.

Pastor Shay takes a shovel and starts to dig a hole at the end of the row of graves. Tommy counts them. Six, seven, eight of them. He slowly walks toward the pastor, wondering for a second who this hole will be for.

Then he has a sudden and awful realization. "Did you know the baby was going to be stillborn?" Tommy asks.

"I knew. He was an innocent."

Shay's words are cut with heavy, frantic breathing.

"I still don't get it. Why would God kill all these people and an innocent baby?"

"He didn't kill them. He took their souls and left their mortal bodies here. The baby didn't get death. He got life."

The scene back there with the wailing mother and the weeping father sure didn't look like *life* to Tommy, but he doesn't say anything to argue. He picks up a shovel to start helping with the hole.

"I was at home having dinner with my family when they all—they were all taken. I didn't know what was happening—and then I heard the first trumpet. The most terrifying thing I think I've ever heard."

Tommy doesn't say anything. He remembers the trumpet blasts all too well.

"I froze when I heard it. I knew instantly. The other trumpet calls just confirmed it. The only thing I could think to do after that was to come here."

Tommy wipes sweat off his forehead and stops for a moment. "I'm sorry for your loss."

"It wasn't my loss. It was their gain."

This sounds like typical pastor talk, though the guy giving it certainly doesn't seem to fit with the typical pastors Tommy has known in his life.

"So why weren't you taken?"

"Just because you have a church and a title doesn't mean you have real faith. I had no relationship, no trust. I just had false comfort. That's how I failed."

Even though he can barely see the pastor's face since the light is behind him, Tommy can tell the man is tearing up. He wants to ask more questions but just can't. He knows Shay is being honest with him, but that doesn't mean he can't be completely out of his freaking mind.

Tommy keeps digging. His tired mind and body are both failing and full of adrenaline. He thinks of the famous movie *The Good, the Bad and the Ugly*. The end where there are only two men left at the cemetery. *"You see, in this world there's two kinds of people, my friend: those with loaded guns, and those who dig. You dig."*

I think I've always been the one digging in my life. I've always been surrounded by people with guns. Dan, Skylar,

Allison, Jack—all of them are gun-toting fools. But not me. I'm the digger. Always have been and always will be.

"Come on, let's finish this hole," Shay says.

Tommy never thought he'd hear such impassionate words being uttered by a pastor.

Then again, he never thought he'd be digging a grave in the basement of a church.

Tommy and Pastor Shay watch as the man holds the small bundle in his hands. It's wrapped in a blanket that was taken from the nursery. This little life never had a chance. It never had an opportunity.

Then again, if Shay is right, all this baby ever had was opportunity. He would never have the chance to grow up and make a mess of things.

Life? Death? What's the difference now that all of this is happening? This in here and out there.

The father bends over and places the bundle in the ground. Then, kneeling before it, he starts to weep. The cries echo in this empty, dark space. Tommy swallows hard and looks away. He wants to leave but he can't. He can't move.

And then Tommy does decide. He wipes tears off his cheeks, feeling the anger curl deep inside him. There is nothing but ugliness here. And the only thing Tommy wants to know is why.

Why?

29
WAITING FOR THE END

Just wait.

So I'm told.

Wait. Then wait a little longer.

Boys will be boys.

It takes them a little longer to grow up.

The games, the nights out, the long days gone, the growing pains.

Just wait, Allison.

So he tells me.

It'll all work out.

So he says.

So I wait. I wait on Jack. Waiting until he's ready for

something more. Waiting because I believe he's the right one. Yet each day that passes strips a little shard from the shell of belief covering me.

Wait.

That's all I do.

I wait.

Allison and Jack sit in a side room off the hallway heading into the church sanctuary. They finally have a chance to be alone and talk and not deal with anything else. At least for these few moments.

"I just wanted to say sorry for how I stormed out of the reception."

Jack's leg touches her and his hand holds hers in a firm grasp that doesn't feel like it will ever let go.

"I'm sorry I was the reason you left."

Considering everything that has happened—all of the death around them combined with the confusion and terror—their argument seems silly and stupid. So many things seem silly and stupid suddenly.

Jack doesn't have his arrogant do-whatever-you-want look on his face like he sometimes does. She's sure she doesn't have that awful witchy look on her face like she knows she does when they argue and she doesn't get her way.

Nobody's getting their way anymore.

"You came looking for me," she says softly. "That's all that matters."

She actually manages to smile, and Jack mirrors it. It's nice to see that smile. She really believed she'd never see it again.

"So when did you start going to this church?" Jack asks her in a sincere manner, not a mocking tone like he might have used hours earlier.

"About six months ago. I don't know. . . . It's not like an every-Sunday thing or anything."

"How come you never told me?"

"I knew you'd laugh," she says with a nervous chuckle. "Laugh and roll your eyes."

"Yeah, you're right. I probably would have. Then."

He takes his other hand and grips her hand tightly with both of his. He suddenly looks very serious and, in a way, sad.

"I don't know what I was waiting for or why it took me so long," Jack says. "I guess I was waiting around for a sign. Like some eureka moment to happen. You just have to make a choice. I realize that. I love you. I *know* that, and I want to marry you."

Jack swallows and then moves out of his seat, bending on one knee while still holding her hands.

What's he doing? Now? He's going to do this now?

She wants to both run out of this room and also rush to embrace him. But Allison does neither. She's just absolutely shocked, more so by this than by anything else that's happened today.

But the moment is suddenly frozen in time.

A banging at the doorway interrupts them, accompanied by "Guys, you need to see this!" shouted by Tommy.

Jack looks at Tommy and is about to say something, but he stands and helps Allison up as well.

Tommy holds his video camera in his hands and motions to it that whatever he has to show them is on it. Allison is half glad for the interruption. She doesn't know what she feels right now. A part of her feels like laughing and another part feels like breaking down to cry. Every inch of her is so full.

Of all the times and all the places . . .

Yet she knew it was probably going to be like this. Things never come at the right time. The moment your parents split up. The moment you lose the love of your life. The moment the world decides to end.

Tommy is cueing up the video. Allison glances briefly at Jack, who has his annoyed look on his face. He spots her looking at him and smiles. She does the same, hesitantly.

The sound of footsteps makes her look at the doorway. She sees the sweaty face of Pastor Shay. "What's going on?" he asks.

"I'm showing them something I just found. Here, come watch this."

"What is it?"

"I was filming—when we were outside—I have it on tape."

"What?" Jack asks.

Tommy keeps pressing buttons until he finally gets to the right moment.

The video starts playing on the small monitor attached to the recorder. It's a scene from outside. Allison sees her friends moving on the street in the murky light. She can't believe how dark it is and how scared everybody looks.

The sound of something like a trumpet wailing in the background overwhelms the camera's tiny speaker. On the screen, everybody stops. The video is jittery and shaking, but Allison can still see clearly enough to make out the terror on Skylar's face.

"The fifth angel sounded his trumpet and opened the Abyss," Pastor Shay says.

The camera is moving as if Tommy was trying to follow the direction of the blaring horns. For a moment they can see only darkness.

"The sun and the sky were darkened and locusts came down upon the earth."

Allison is not sure what the pastor is referring to. She can see Skylar back on the screen, looking all around her until—

She's grabbed by something and disappears.

No no no.

"Whoa," they all collectively gasp.

"What the—?" Jack starts to say.

"And were given power like that of scorpions of the earth," Pastor Shay finishes.

Tommy rewinds a bit and then pauses.

There's something Allison can make out in the darkness. Some kind of strange shadow hovering right over Skylar. It's like the night suddenly grew teeth and pulled her into the thick black.

They stare at the freaky image.

"They had hair like women's hair, and their teeth were like lions' teeth," Pastor Shay says. "The sound of their wings was like the thundering of many horses rushing into battle."

If it were up to Allison she'd tell the pastor to shut up. He's really freaking her out. But she can't. She's afraid to.

"Look at this," Tommy says as he starts zooming in on the shape. It's blurry with the pixels having a hard time forming the outline, but she can make out something.

What is that?

Jack curses.

Allison feels goosebumps. Whatever they're looking at—this dimly lit *thing*—it's terrifying. She can make out stringy hair and long wings and an even longer tail.

That thing is grotesque.

It's something out of a nightmare. Something terrifying. Something unimaginable.

"They had tails with stingers, like scorpions, and they had the power to torment people."

"Okay, now you're just freaking us all out," Jack says to the pastor. "What are you talking about? And what is that thing?"

"One of the fallen," Shay tells them. "The opposite of life."

"You talking demons?" Allison asks.

The pastor nods.

Wonderful.

"What do they want?" Jack asks.

It's not a question of whether there's really anything there. They all know now there's something there.

"To torture. To destroy."

I'm glad I'm not a full-time member of your church, Pastor Doom and Gloom.

"There's got to be a way to fight them," Jack says.

Tommy just stands there, the implications of this discovery clear on his face. Allison knows he'd normally be beaming with pride, but there's not one ounce of it on Tommy's face. Just bleak terror.

They all wait for the pastor to explain more. "This is the first season of bad things to come."

"The first?" Tommy asks.

Shay nods and looks at them without any sort of reaction. It's like he's known this was coming for years. "It's going to get worse," the pastor tells them in a low, no-nonsense manner.

Allison glances at Jack, who just stares ahead at the pastor.

Maybe she doesn't need to worry about waiting for a proposal anymore. Maybe that's been the reason all along. It was never meant to happen because the end was near.

And now, the end doesn't look just near. It's scratching at the window waiting to come in.

Waiting to come in and prick the life out of every single one of them.

30
THE SCREAMING SOUL

Tommy sits in the padded pew going through his video recorder to see if there's anything else that sticks out at him. But all he can really think of is what he saw back there in the room right before he interrupted them.

Jack was about to pop the big question to Allison.

All it took was the end of the world. Nice to know.

Note to self: Maybe don't wait until the end of the world to let the people you care for know about it.

Jack was on his knees—literally on his knees—about to ask Allison to marry him.

Tommy wonders if Allison would have said yes. Does

it really matter anyway? But if it doesn't, then why did he stop Jack from asking?

I mean, where would they get married and who would be left alive to even come to the wedding?

These crazy thoughts swirl around his head until he hears someone come and sit beside him. He looks up and sees Sam's dyed-white hair. For a moment she makes sure she's not interrupting something important.

"I just heard a news report," Sam finally says. "Churches are being attacked."

"Attacked by who?"

"Not who; what. Aliens, demons, whatever. Like the thing that attacked your friend."

"Where'd you hear it?" he asks.

"Someone has a radio. No cell phones are working. The televisions aren't showing anything and the Internet's down. But there's a few radio stations still broadcasting."

Tommy glances around the room. Nobody seems very social. Most people are keeping to themselves or are huddled in groups of two and three. Tommy's spoken with a few of them just to try and learn as much as he can.

"People are talking about leaving in the morning," he says. "Getting out of the city."

"You think we should go?"

He notices the word *we*. But she's a part of their group now, like it or not. Tommy stares up at the cross in the center of the wall behind the pulpit. "I don't know. Maybe. Might be a good idea, especially if some crazy monster is going to attack us here if we stay in the church." He can hardly believe the words coming out of his own mouth.

This is nuts.

The door in the corner behind the organ opens and Jack comes walking out. He makes his way to Tommy.

You better not be engaged.

Jack greets them both.

"You see Skylar?" Tommy asks.

Jack nods. "Just now."

"How's she doing?"

"She's okay. Allie and Dan are back there with her."

Tommy nods, staring up at the stained-glass window. He keeps seeing the shadowy thing from the video taking Skylar into its arms (or tentacles or whatever they were).

"Did you see that? I mean—what was that thing that attacked her?"

Jack looks like he's in a daze. He only shakes his head, staring back at the people in the church. "I don't know. . . ."

If Tommy had to say what he was feeling deep down, he'd be forced to admit that Pastor Shay was probably right. The Rapture. The end of the world. Maybe Jack would say the same thing—the look on his friend's face seems to confirm it. But neither of them seems to want to say it out loud yet. It's still too wild, too crazy, too . . .

Horrific.

"What do you think we should do?" Tommy asks.

"Hole up here," Jack says.

"Until what? Sam says churches are being attacked by those things. Some of the people around here are planning on leaving in the morning."

Jack scans the room. "Oh, really? And go where? We don't know for sure what's happening out there. At least in here it seems like we're safe."

"So you want to just sit here and see what happens?" *We've found Allison. Now we can escape this dungeon.*

"Till we figure out a better plan, Tommy."

Tommy shrugs, still feeling that caged-in sensation. "Maybe we should move on, see if—"

"To where?" Jack interrupts. "Anyway, we can't move Skylar."

Tommy is going to answer when a screeching sound outside does it for him. They both stand up and look toward the front of the sanctuary.

Another scream pierces the stillness. Some of the survivors in the room gather around Tommy and Jack.

"What was that?" Tommy asks.

Another sound, this one lower and darker and louder, comes from the front of the church. It's like the sound of the undead, the sound of something unholy, unreal—and the sound is approaching.

It's rushing toward the screaming sounds. Someone outside is being attacked.

The demonic sound is suddenly above them, hovering and howling and moving.

The screaming human outside abruptly stops.

No.

The hunter found its prey.

We have to leave this place we're surrounded and they're just watching us waiting for us at any moment.

Sam comes close to Tommy and he puts an arm around her. *You were right.* The group in the church stand together, not making a sound, not moving.

Everybody Tommy can see looks absolutely terrified.

I wonder if I look just like them.

He breathes in and out slowly, not sure when the next sound will come, not sure where it will come from.

A smashing sound comes from the stained-glass window. A figure crawling—no, *thrown* against it—sends the glass cracking in a thousand little spiderwebs.

"God, help me!" the figure cries out. "Oh, no! Please, no!"

Suddenly the body is sucked back up and out and away from the window and the church.

Everybody darts toward the back of the sanctuary, getting away from the glass and the monsters that hover outside it. Tommy wishes he could assure them that they're safe, but he doesn't feel safe in any way. He's cursing in his mind and wondering how in the world they can get out of here now.

They know we're in here. They've heard us and probably seen us or felt us.

Now what?

That's the question.

Will we each be picked off one by one like the poor,

unfortunate screaming soul outside? Ripped and tossed about like they did to Skylar?

That's not going to happen to us. We're going to fight back.

Tommy looks around. He just sees a bunch of frightened and unfamiliar faces. Even Jack looks defeated and weary.

"It's going to be okay," Tommy says to any of them.

But he's not sure any of them are listening.

31
UNDERTOW

"Mommy?"

"What, Sky?"

"Why didn't I have any sisters?"

"'Cause God decided that you were enough."

"Did you and Dad want more kids?"

"Of course."

"Are you sad that you didn't have any more?"

"No. You're like having three girls."

"That doesn't sound so good."

"We were blessed with you, Skylar. You were an answer to many prayers. You still are."

Memories and conversations drift by like eyelids closing over her heart and soul. Skylar continues to feel the slow and steady dropping of everything: her energy, her emotions, her breathing, her resistance to the pain. With each breath, some little bit of her hurts more. Her body is so cold and continues to shake even though she's damp with sweat. Her bones throb as if the flesh is being flayed off them. She'll close her eyes and remember something random, like this conversation she had with her mother when she was just a little girl. Strange things that she hasn't thought about for years.

That's because I'm dying and this is what happens when your body declines.

Dan has been at her side the whole time. She's been moved to another room without any other patients. She lies on a cot while Dan places a fresh, cold rag on her burning forehead.

The nurse comes in to check on her. "How do you feel?"

She wants to laugh and ask, "How do you think I feel?"

The world decided to end on her wedding day. Not just start to come apart, but *end.*

Her parents and one of her best friends are dead. Not sick but gone. Bye-bye.

Some demon thing grabbed her and stuck her in the back and now she's dying because of it.

So yeah, I'm doing great, how are you doing?

"I've been better," she tells Rachel through teeth that can't stop chattering.

The room occasionally spins and Dan alternately looks

close and then far away. She knows she's seeing things and feeling things and this is all part of the bad thing that happens to dying people.

She opens her eyes again and sees Dan's sweet, innocent gaze, the kind that made her fall in love with him. The kind that looks like it's about to break into a hundred million pieces right now.

A fresh wave of pain crashes into her.

"Please, Dan," she gets out. "Please."

"What is it?"

"I can't take this. The pain. I'm burning. Please. Make it stop."

He squeezes her hand. "No. Just—hold on. Breathe."

Her stomach feels like a car is driving over it. Very slowly riding over it. Back and forth. This pressure that makes her feel like she can't breathe. This crazy, awful aching.

"I want you to do something for me," she tells Dan. "Kill me. Please."

"Stop," Dan tells her. "It's going to be okay."

Skylar can see the somber look on the nurse's face. Her eyes close again for a brief moment.

She can picture herself riding down the street on her old bike. So light, so carefree, the sky up above endless and warm and so inviting.

Nothing terrible could ever come from those beautiful heavens above, right?

Where are You, God? Why are You doing this?

"I've given her the last dose of Vicodin we have," Nurse Rachel tells Dan. Then she turns to talk to her. "Your pain should come down a little bit soon, sweetie."

"It's burning. I feel like I'm in the middle of a forest fire and I still can't stop this shaking. Please—I can't—it's just too much. Please . . ."

As she closes her eyes again, this time she pictures something else. Something awful. A black, breathing specter in the shadows, smiling with bloodstained teeth, piercing her and shaking her and ready to kill her.

Dan looks at her and says softly, "I'm sorry."

Skylar reaches for something and finds the lantern. In a blind, delirious fury, she imagines grabbing it and slamming it against Dan's head. Instead she can barely keep the lantern steady in her grasp. Dan reaches out and takes it from her.

"Kill me," she screams out.

Nobody is listening to her, so maybe that'll get their attention.

She's suffocating and roasting and losing her mind here.

Please just spare me get me out of here take this all of this away please Dan please God please.

But they just stand there, over her, like she's some kind of rat, some kind of anonymous patient, some kind of stranger.

"It's getting infected," the nurse tells Dan. "We don't have antibiotics."

"Dan," Skylar almost spits out as she fights to keep

her teeth from chipping away at each other. "Please, Dan, help me."

Her eyes close but she fights, hanging on, still hearing them talk, still thinking she's alive even though she doesn't want to be anymore.

"Where can I get the medicine she needs?" her husband asks.

My man my husband my main squeeze the love of my life the life that is only moments from ending.

"My minivan," the nurse says. "I have sample packets of penicillin. But it's too dangerous to go out there."

Skylar wants to interject.

I'll go. Just give me the car keys and I'll go. I can't even feel my legs and my stomach feels like one giant bee keeps stinging it over and over again but it's okay I'll go.

"Give me the keys," Dan says.

Skylar doesn't know if she's imagining this. Maybe all of this. Maybe she bumped her head during the bridal dance. Yeah, maybe that's what happened and this is all some long, drawn-out bridal nightmare.

"It's not safe out there," Rachel says.

"You want to go out there with those things?" another voice says.

This one sounds like Tommy.

Tommy, Tommy, Tommy.

Please film this, Tommy. Get a close-up of my chattering teeth and sweating face and dying eyes. Please. It'll go great with your documentary on the end of the world.

More voices come, but it doesn't matter. She's slowly fading away, either to sleep or a coma or death.

Something soft brushes against her feet. Actually, she's sinking in wet sand. The ocean waves glide over her. She can feel herself drifting in the waters, the tug of the undertow starting to pull her farther and farther out.

It's called death the black boogeyman the grim reaper and he's finally come to get me.

Voices in the distance mumble away.

"I'll show you," someone says.

"Don't do this," another one says.

"We got this," another voice calls out.

"Let's go."

She feels a kiss on her forehead and Skylar finally disappears.

32
MINIVAN COFFIN

"I'm going to head out there with Dan to find Skylar some medicine."

Tommy's words are directed to Jack and Allison, but really he's just talking to Allie. He wanted to show her something, anything. To be the hero. To be able to do something. To maybe cause some kind of reaction. But instead, his two friends just tell him to be careful.

A minute later, standing in the front of the church by the locked door that's been barricaded, Tommy can feel his adrenaline flowing. He might be outside two minutes before one of those things takes him. He has no idea. He wishes he could see Allison's face one more time but she stayed back there with Skylar. Dan is next to him, fired up and ready to go as well.

This might be completely foolish.

Yet this isn't some kind of swimming-in-the-lake-when-a-serial-killer-is-near sort of moment. Skylar is dying and they have to do something.

It's obvious why Dan is going. For Tommy, he can't stay still any longer. Just like videoing the wedding, Tommy has to be doing something. Otherwise he'll just be going crazy feeling like he's worthless.

He stares at the nurse, who looks more calm than anybody else Tommy has seen. She's giving Dan and him instructions. Nearby, Sam and Jack stand listening, wanting to know if they can do anything as well.

"It's a green Dodge minivan and it got blocked in on Sixth Street, just out of the parking lot. There was an SUV near me, I think—"

"You think?" Tommy asks.

The nurse just gives him a stern, pipe-down-son sort of look. "I was jammed in."

Her tone tells Tommy all he needs to know. He just nods, apologizing for his snarky comment.

"We'll find it."

"Keys?" Dan asks, holding out his hand to Rachel.

The tension between Rachel and Tommy goes away when she hands Dan the keys. Tommy knows she's just like everybody else—confused and going out of her mind. It's just, he and Dan are about to go out there and possibly get killed. He doesn't need to state the obvious, of course. But he also needs a little help in here. From everybody he can get it from.

Jack puts his hand on Tommy's shoulder. "You sure you don't want me to go?"

"We're good," Dan says.

Tommy wants to object.

Yeah, actually, you go and I'll stay back here and watch over Allison. I mean Skylar.

But Tommy only nods in agreement.

His heart is pounding. It's racing so hard it's almost pushing him out this church door.

"The sample packets of amoxicillin are in a duffel bag in the back of the van."

They nod at her, then look at each other.

"Man, I really don't want to die in the back of a minivan with you," Tommy says, trying to add some humor.

Dan gives a faint smile, looking as nervous as Tommy feels. Then they open up the door and head outside to God knows what.

The night feels raw. Like something's been torn off it and it's sitting there all bloody and infected. It's colder and the sky is darker and the air feels like a blank screen of static. Tommy glances at the closed and locked door of the church and immediately wants to go back inside.

We are really doing this. We're really being the brave ones and going on a night journey for medicine.

The sidewalk feels exceptionally hard under his feet. For a moment, he stands next to Dan, both of them staying put as they survey the silent night around them. A lone streetlamp casts an eerie glow around them.

"You sure about this?" he asks Dan.

The question seems to snap Dan out of his fearful stance. He gives a stern nod.

We're out here for Skylar.

Tommy wonders if those things out there are long-winged beasts like the kind out of the Lord of the Rings saga. Perhaps they'll show up and grab both of them with long, piercing claws. Maybe they'll get sucked up into the night sky and never be seen again.

"Let's go," Dan tells him.

They start down the sidewalk to the edge of the street. Tommy sees the endless line of parked cars stuck in the gloomy shadows like coffins lined up in rows of death.

I'm not looking inside those cars.

But Tommy can't help seeing some of them. There's broken glass everywhere and a spattering of something dark covers the sides of a few of the cars.

As they weave their way through the two rows of cars, Tommy begins to hear the sound of millions of crickets and bugs. They seem to be stuck in every hole and corner in this otherwise abandoned city. It's a hellish sort of humming, vibrating from the pit of somewhere dark and disturbing.

His heart beats.

Just keep going don't think about it.

The moon can be seen but even it looks different, the cold light not so bright. It looks like it's more reddish-gray than white.

They cross an intersection, making sure nobody and nothing is in sight before proceeding. They hide for a moment in an enclosed doorway, then keep making it down the sidewalk. Then they're back on the street, on Sixth Street going between more coffin-cars.

The crash of broken glass sounds behind them. They stop and look. Tommy feels smothered by the cars, their jammed-in positions making him claustrophobic.

The sound came from a figure in the night, a man breaking into a car to get something. They see him pulling out a water bottle and then placing it in a shopping cart on the sidewalk. Tommy shakes his head and looks at Dan, who's staring down the street in the opposite direction.

"You hear that?" Dan asks.

Tommy nods, looking at the survivor who is now pushing his cart toward the shadows and emptiness of the night.

"He broke the car window," Tommy says.

"No, no, over there," Dan says. "There's something there."

The moonlight and few streetlights play tricks with his eyes. It feels like the ruby glow is shaking, quivering almost.

Tommy looks back at the stranger with the shopping cart.

"You need to get inside where it's safe," he tells the man. "It's safer in the church."

Blank eyes look back at him. They don't act like they've heard him. If they did, they sure don't care.

"I see the van," Dan tells him.

They begin to head toward the van when a howling, sick sound cries out behind them. For a minute, Tommy thinks it's the stranger they passed.

Maybe it is. Or maybe it's the thing that—GO!

Tommy breathes in. He doesn't just walk now. They're rushing through the cars trying to get to the van as fast as possible.

Another sound. A screeching, breaking, tearing sound piercing the darkness behind them.

They approach the van.

"Unlock it," Tommy shouts at his friend.

Dan's hand is moving but nothing is happening.

"It's not opening."

No.

This is how they die.

This is how the end snatches them from behind.

The stupid minivan door opener doesn't work.

A car alarm a few cars behind them goes off like a siren with the lights barking on and off. Dan is still trying to unlock the van.

The keys in Dan's hand give Tommy an idea. He grabs them and holds them up, pressing the unlock button.

A chirping sound and the lights of a van several cars over blink once.

They both look at each other.

This was the wrong van.

Tommy smiles at Dan in disbelief as they both break off and dash toward the van.

The sound behind them roars like a demented animal that's been set free from its cage. It's like nothing Tommy has ever heard and he knows it's something he never wants to hear again.

He just wants to get off these streets and out of this city.

He misses the church more than ever now.

33
ATTACKED

"I want to explore the world."

"Don't you want to find someone special? Settle down. Buy a dog."

"I'll let Skylar and you do that."

"I'm telling you, Tommy, you gotta think about the future."

"What for? I'll wait till tomorrow. I just want to enjoy today. You know?"

"You can enjoy today and still plan ahead."

"I don't want a spreadsheet on my goals for the next ten years. I want things to just happen. I want to figure it out when I get there."

"And you'll film it all along the way?"

"I'll try. There's a lot of beautiful things to capture. I just can't wait."

"For what?"

"To see what's round the corner. To go to far-off places and come back and visit Skylar and you and all the babies you're going to have."

"Will you babysit?"

"Absolutely . . . not."

The late-night conversation over some beers outside on a summer night feels like a universe away. The ease of the evening and the naiveté behind his statements seem to mock Tommy now.

The memory is a little flicker of a spark inside this dark place. He recalls it and then wonders what in the world he was thinking. Not a care in life and a full belief that he'd go out into the world and see it and find someone and find a place and his part in it.

Meaningless.

Meaningless because he's now racing down a street full of abandoned cars, trying to stay clear of . . . something. Some horrific thing out there.

They reach the minivan and climb inside and shut the doors.

Okay, good. We're inside. We're safe for the moment.

Along with the blaring car alarm outside, Tommy hears Dan's heavy breathing and stares at him, seeing his friend sitting there in his tuxedo. The end of the world comes and they're still in their formal attire. Tommy's already tired of the dress shoes he's wearing. He makes a note to find some different clothes fast.

The alarm suddenly goes silent. Everything seems to just stop. Like someone putting a finger over the lips of this city. A gigantic hush smothers over them. The kind that suffocates. The kind you don't wake up from.

Dan doesn't wait. He moves to the back of the van and starts rummaging through the clutter. Tommy looks and sees the items Dan tosses behind him—a bag of tennis racquets, a duffel bag full of workout attire, some wrapped presents. The car's interior is dark, and Dan tries to turn on the dome light above him, but no light comes on.

"Turn on the power," he tells Tommy. "I need some light. I can't find the bag. She's got so much junk back here."

Tommy puts the key in the ignition and the sound of static on the radio rips through the van, freaking him out a bit. Dan is able to turn on the light to see what he's doing. While he does that, Tommy tries to find anything on the radio. He searches and soon hears the distant, tinny voice of a man who sounds like an old preacher talking.

"There was no terrorist attack, no viral outbreak—there are millions of dead, all around us. All the children are dead. There is no doubt in my mind this was the Rapture—"

"Turn it off," Dan shouts at him.

Sounds good to me. Tommy douses the car in silence once again.

Dan is still bent over, looking through everything at the back of the minivan. For a moment, Tommy can't get the old-timer's voice out of his head. He's curious what the guy is going to keep talking about, so he turns the radio back on but keeps the volume low.

"You need to understand that there is only one way to God—only one way to eternal life. You listen to me! Stop what you're doing, get down on your knees, and pray this prayer with me—and believe it."

"Yes," Dan shouts out.

Dan is holding up a bag—it must be the amoxicillin. Tommy nods and gives him a thumbs-up but still listens to the man on the radio. He's curious. He wants to hear what this nut-job says to do.

Blame it on the Rapture. How convenient.

"You first need to confess that you're a sinner, and that—"

Tommy's head slams into the steering wheel as something pounds the front of the minivan. He can hear Dan yelling as his friend is launched into the back of a seat. Holding his forehead, Tommy looks at Dan. He can see the expression on his friend's face.

It's the same look he must have.

They're here.

Whatever *they* might be.

Aliens or devils or terrorists or some kind of monster he doesn't know about.

Whatever they might be, calling this the Rapture and praying isn't going to do anything.

Getting out of here is what we need to do.

Dan kneels on the floor of the van and reaches up quickly to turn off the light. Not that it's going to help.

"Did you see anything?" he asks Tommy.

Tommy moves to the back of the minivan, looking out the window toward the street and the other sleeping vehicles. There's nothing out there—no movement, no shape, nothing. He looks out the side window. He hears a low hum outside from something but sees nothing.

He wipes the sweat from his forehead. His temple still hurts from bashing into the steering wheel. Then he looks out the windshield.

"It hit the front of the van," Tommy says in a hushed voice.

Any minute something might jump out at them. Anything.

A cold hand grabbing his thigh.

A warm, moist palm sliding against his cheek.

Teeth ripping into his shoulder.

Enough, Tommy.

Dan is beside him now and he's looking through the windshield too. They both watch and wait.

The window fogs up.

How's that happening?

It feels like—any second now—whatever is out there . . .

Get on your knees now or you're gonna die you're gonna get what you deserve you're gonna suffer you miserable sinner.

They can't see out the front window anymore. Dan moves forward, trying to see what's outside.

A piercing boom, and glass rains all over them as the windows explode and the minivan shakes.

Tommy curses when something—*some thing some monster some kind of something*—lands on the roof, blowing out the side and back windows.

Then they see it: the imprint in the roof just above their heads. It looks sort of like a . . . talon. Belonging to a massive bird.

But of course that's crazy, right, just like the end of the world being crazy and Skylar's parents dying right in front of me and Lauren dying and everybody dying or leaving this city.

The van begins to rock back and forth. Harder and harder. Tommy grabs the door handle as the shaking continues.

Then he sees something like a tentacle on the outside, moving and wiggling and shaking right outside the window lined with broken shards of glass.

It's a tail.

Everything happens in violent fast motion while somehow being on slow-mo at the same time. Dan is next to him, hunkering down and trying to keep from being stabbed or stuck or struck by whatever that thing might be.

The voice on the radio seems to get louder now, the preacher yelling out his message of hope.

The van continues to shake.

We're going to die right now. That thing is going to swallow us whole.

The preacher doesn't seem scared one bit, however.

"Back to hell with you, demon!" the man on the radio shouts out.

The van suddenly stops shaking.

The violent thrashing is over.

Tommy looks at Dan, who is right next to him. He wants to say something but can't. He doesn't know what to say and is afraid it might bring that thing back if he makes a single sound.

All Tommy wants to do is get out of this van.

He closes his eyes for a moment, trying to regain enough strength and courage to get out of here and run back into the church. When he opens them again, he sees the shell-shocked survivor from earlier—the window breaker with the shopping cart. The man appears enraged as he stands in front of the minivan, looking on top of the roof.

The thing must still be there.

"You're no match for God!" the man cries out. "The power of Christ compels you!"

Tommy doesn't know what to do. He just sits and watches the man.

Suddenly there's a quick rattling, and then the imprint on the roof disappears.

"It's gone," Tommy says in a voice of exasperated relief.

They both look at each other and know what needs to happen.

The back doors open and they climb out.

"Run," Dan shouts as he holds the bag full of medicine.

Tommy is almost out of the van when he hears the scream. It sounds like someone choking on something while howling at the top of his lungs. He can't help but turn back and see the man who was just hollering out in the night air being slammed against the front window.

No!

The van shakes again and the radio goes silent. Tommy is out now and looks back one more time.

The stranger on the street is now being lifted up and over the van.

This is crazy this is crazy.

He's seen enough and so have his legs and his body. Now he's sprinting and trying to avoid the cars and trying to stay close to Dan and hoping that the winged beast with the massive talons doesn't swoop in and claw him up.

As the screams behind them continue, Tommy and Dan race back to the church. The car alarms begin to all go off now. They're being hounded and harassed and chased.

The church is just up ahead.

They're almost there.

Almost there.

Almost . . .

34
THE BIG QUESTION

The sand still between my toes.

The sea and the surf a stone's throw from the balcony.

The sun fading fast. Too fast.

Mom tries to explain but her words still sound hollow.

"I thought we were doing the right thing. I thought I was doing the right thing."

"It doesn't matter, does it?"

"Yes, Allie—it does matter. It matters more than you realize."

"I'm just not interested. It only brings more confusion than hope."

"Your father doesn't want to have anything to do with God,

but I've come to rely on him. It's the only thing I can rely on these days."

The orange glow that hovers over us will be gone soon. So will Mom. So will these talks about God and faith. So will the bothersome pricks in my side.

I don't need them anymore.

There was a time, but it's gone. It's passed.

Allison remembers the conversation with her mother and how she was convinced that her time with God and her parents' faith—no, actually her mother's faith—was done. How it was a thing in her past. But lately, that past has come to mind more and more. That's why she came here in the first place. To be reminded of it. To find hope inside it. To seek some kind of answer in the pews of this church.

Yet as each moment passes, all she finds is that same empty feeling that seems to follow her wherever she goes.

She doesn't want to live with this feeling anymore. And she definitely doesn't want to die with it.

Allison wanders down a hallway into an open area that has a stairwell and another doorway leading to the outside. She spots Jack looking out one of the windows into the dark night.

"See anything?" she asks simply to start a conversation.

She knows he hasn't seen anything since there's nothing to see.

"There's nobody on the streets. No passing cars. Nothing."

Jack has been restless ever since Tommy and Dan left a while ago.

"They'll be back soon," Allison says, trying to encourage.

"They've been gone a long time."

"It'll be okay."

Jack turns and looks at her. So far they still haven't really talked since they were interrupted earlier. They've circled around the things that really need to be spoken about, but the right moment just hasn't come. Allison has been with Skylar most of the time since then.

"I better get back to the main entrance," he says. "In case they arrive."

"Jack . . ."

She wonders if he's ever going to finish their earlier conversation. She knows where he was heading and what he sounded like he was going to ask.

They stare at one another for a moment, so much said between them in a simple look.

Everything seems different now. Everything.

Maybe it doesn't matter anyway. Married or not. The end is here and they probably only have days left, hours maybe.

Then maybe it matters even more.

"I'm nervous," he says. "I should've gone with them."

"It wouldn't help if all three of you weren't here."

He sighs and nods.

"I thought—when I was here by myself and then everything started to happen—all I could think was how much I wished I was back at the hotel."

"You're lucky you weren't there," Jack says, his voice so somber and weak. "All the dead bodies everywhere. Everybody losing their mind. It was chaos."

"It's chaos everywhere."

"Yeah. It just seems worse when you're surrounded. By the living and the dead."

She thinks of that conversation with her mother a year ago, the one where she told Allison about her newfound faith and how helpful it had been. Allison wants to share this with Jack. She's wanted to share things like this with him for a while.

"Come on—let's go and see if they're back," Jack tells her.

He puts an arm around her and it's comforting. This light, casual touch. Something she took for granted before all of this happened.

I won't take it for granted again. Ever.

But sometimes you wait to appreciate something only to find it permanently gone.

Relief comes in the form of screaming and knocking at the door.

Dan and Tommy have made it.

There's a rush and a whirlwind to get the two guys back

inside, with Jack pulling away the tables and chairs put there for security and Pastor Shay unbolting the door. Dan and Tommy are pale and sweaty and look terrified as they spill through the door. Allison doesn't see the bag Dan is holding at first, and for a moment she's disheartened. But then Dan, still sucking in air and bent over, holds out the bag for Rachel. The nurse takes it after giving him a hug in greeting.

The two young men share a look of triumph even though it's short-lived. Dan follows the nurse back to the room where Skylar is. Allison stays with Jack and Tommy and the others. They wait to hear what happened.

"Something is out there," Tommy tells them, sounding like he's getting ready to tell a ghost story.

If only it could be so harmless.

"What is it?" Jack asks.

"I have no idea," Tommy says, still breathing heavily and wiping his forehead with the sleeve of his dress shirt. "Some kind of monster. Something awful."

Tommy's never been one to exaggerate. Joke around, sure, but not talk with terror lacing his tone.

"It attacked us. It blew out the windows of the minivan."

"But what was it?" Jack asks.

"I just saw its tail or maybe one of its . . . claws or something."

Jack looks disbelieving.

Tommy shakes his head, tired and obviously not interested in trying to debate what he saw.

"Are you okay?" Allison asks him.

Tommy gives her an odd look and just nods. Then he walks back into the sanctuary. Jack looks serious and begins to stack the chairs and tables on top of one another to barricade the front doors again.

Allison stands in the foyer, feeling cold and empty and helpless.

But the boys are still alive, a voice reminds her. *They came back.*

Hope is not gone.

Hope is still out there.

That's exactly what her mother told her once.

So what does she think now?

The big question. Yesterday, today, and tomorrow. If tomorrow does indeed come.

35
THE TICKING CLOCK

A new group of strangers arrives in the church, and one of them carries scenes from the maelstrom outside. A man was able to save some videos he found online before the connection broke. Now a group surrounds the piano while the man's tablet stands upon it and shows the video.

They play it again because it's too unreal to take in the first time. It doesn't look natural.

Tommy is in the middle of the group of strangers, watching. At first he was trying to figure out how they got an Internet connection when he's been trying ever since getting here. But his phone is dead now anyway, so it doesn't matter. The tablet's owner says these videos were downloaded from YouTube just hours ago.

The first video reveals a stretch of beach. To Tommy it looks like the Atlantic. Then he realizes the person who posted this video is from California, so it has to be the West Coast. The shaky video shows the ocean, or where the ocean used to be, with its dried-up shore lined with dead sea life. Thousands of dead fish and sharks and dolphins cover the sand. The ocean seems to be receding and drying up.

Death is everywhere.

Not just in this video, but in this world.

Someone says the obvious. "It's happening everywhere."

Tommy doesn't want to believe it. He thinks about this video and then realizes the importance of the video he's taken.

I need to figure out a way to show it, too. To get it online. To help let people know . . .

But he can't finish the rest of that thought.

Help them know what, Tommy? That the world is over? That they might as well wave the white flag and put a gun in their mouth and blow off their head?

A Radiohead song comes to mind. He wishes he could have his iPod and just crank it up and let everything else fade away. But it doesn't work like that. Not here and now.

Separating like ripples on a black shore.

The separation has finally come and those ripples are everywhere. The shores are all black as the night. Tommy wonders what tomorrow will bring, if the sun will rise and if they will see some kind of daylight.

If we make it to tomorrow.

"There's more," the man says to them like someone announcing that the volcano has erupted and the lava is only seconds away.

A cell phone video plays. It's a peewee basketball game with the young boys and girls running up and down the court, barely knowing which way to go. The person filming obviously has to be a proud parent zooming in on his boy.

Then it's blurry and there's rumbling and screaming.

"Oh no! No!" the adult voice screams.

The video zooms out and focuses back on the court. All the kids are now littering the court, dead and scattered like garbage. The screams magnify as more parents freak out.

All the kids—every one is dead. Taken. Tossed about.

Then the video shows the stands, where a few adults lie dead as well.

Another video shows a park with corpses strewn throughout it. A mother lies dead behind a toddler swing, her newborn still swaying slightly in it, eyes white and gone.

And there's more.

A police video where a man's being cuffed until the cop collapses behind him.

A traffic-jam video that resembles the mess Tommy and Dan were just in.

There's even a scene at a small diner where several patrons suddenly drop dead and a waitress crumples to the floor. Then it shows a cook resting on a searing grill, the man's hands and face and chest all grilling along with the burgers he was just cooking.

This is madness.

The group of strangers continue to talk but Tommy slips away. He's seen enough. The videos are reminders.

Time is short. I might be gone tomorrow. Or tonight.

He needs to do something and do it fast. So he heads somewhere private. Goodness knows this church is big enough to find a room that's not occupied.

So many rooms to house the dead. Wonder if it held this many living folks when they were around to come in through the doors.

The sound of his feet on the carpet seems too loud. The echoes of his steps seem too empty. Tommy's mind keeps going back to the desolate seashore with all the dead fish everywhere.

So Jesus fed the five thousand but what about here what about now?

Anger rips inside of him. He sees a cross every ten feet he walks, it seems. It's ridiculous. God is not here. He's not in this building and he's surely not outside. He's not watching. If he's up there, he's shut the door and locked it.

We are all out there on that receding ocean in a tiny boat that's leaking and sinking. We're all sinking and we're all forgotten.

He remembers another Radiohead lyric.

"I'm not here. This isn't happening."

But Tommy *is* here and this *definitely* is happening. No

going back. No turning around. No starting over again. No time for being a sissy.

No time. No time whatsoever.

So it's time to do this one thing.

Moments later, he's got everything set up. The room is upstairs and nobody is around. His video camera is on a desk while he's sitting in a chair, eating peanut butter off a knife. The jar he found is on the floor.

He's been interviewing everybody else today. Now it's his turn.

The clock is ticking get it over with.

"My name is Tommy Covington," he says directly into the camera. "If you're watching this I'm probably dead."

He takes a bite of the peanut butter. Strangely, it calms him a bit, not only eating something but doing something so natural. He looks at his watch, which does happen to still be working. At least for the time being.

"It's been ten hours since it started. We've made it to a church and have found some help, but if something happens, Allie, I need to say this to you."

He hears the door squeak open and sees Sam entering the room. She's holding her phone on him as if she's filming. He stands up and shakes his head, going to turn off his camera for the moment.

Can't a guy have a single private second around here?

"Uh-uh, turn it off," he tells her, holding up a hand.

"What? Why?"

"I don't like people filming me."

Sam smiles. "Says the guy filming everyone."

He laughs, then shrugs and puts the knife back into the peanut butter jar to have one last bite. He doesn't really want Sam knowing anything, so he's going to play it off and be cool and calm in front of her.

Sam gives him a curious look. "So what's so important you need to tell Allie?"

Tommy slides the knife back into his mouth. A full mouth is better than having to answer that question. Still, Sam doesn't appear like she's going to let him off the hook.

"It's complicated," he eventually tells her.

The Goth girl taps her phone off and stops aiming it at him. She gives him a cheerful, friendly smile. "Don't you think fire and ice falling from the sky should uncomplicate things?"

Tommy moves his tongue around his mouth to get the remaining peanut butter unstuck. "Probably."

Sam picks up his camera. "Then tell her what you wanted to say. I'll get it to her if something happens."

How come this young girl knows so much when Allie doesn't have a clue?

He wonders if he's said or done anything to make it obvious. He stands for a moment, contemplating taking his camera and his thoughts and keeping them all to himself. "I . . . I can't, Sam. Not now."

"You want her *never* to know?" Sam asks.

She turns on the video recorder and aims it at him. Tommy feels frozen for the moment.

She has a good point. I want her to know and I want her to know now.

He wonders what's the worst thing that could happen. Hasn't it already happened?

Okay, fine.

"Allie, if something happens to me I want you to know this," he begins to say, each word feeling easier to say than the last. "When Jack gave that toast, my stomach twisted into a thousand knots."

Tommy stares down at the floor for a moment, searching his thoughts. So many words to say and so not the way he wanted to say them.

"At first, it was because I felt bad for you," Tommy continues, looking back up at the camera. "But then it was because I realized he was right."

He moves closer to the camera, imagining that he's talking to Allison and looking her directly in the eyes. He can see them. All he has to do is blink and they're there.

"I know that because when I met you seven years ago, we just clicked, and over time I knew you were the one for me. I just knew."

He pauses.

Don't hold back because time isn't on your side. Time was never on your side and it certainly isn't anymore.

"Truth is, I've loved you every day since. And if it's not me you're meant to be with, I just want you to be happy."

He looks away at Sam and then nods for her to stop filming.

"Feel better?"

"Yeah."

It's a strange thing to say out loud something you've kept silent and tucked away for years. To articulate words you weren't exactly sure about, to voice them and hear how they sound on your lips. Tommy knows that they were only spoken for the camera and not for Allison, but still, it's something. It means something.

He glances at the empty peanut butter jar in his hand. "You hungry, Sam?"

36
THE GREAT GENERAL IN THE SKY

She sees the snow all around her swirling and streaming. Going upward and sideways and every which way, surrounding her. Skylar holds out her hands with joy in her heart and a smile on her face until she realizes it's not soft snow she's touching. It's locusts. Squirming, crackling little locusts that suddenly turn from white to black as they swarm around her, suffocating, strangling . . .

Skylar opens her eyes, yet the dream remains.

I have found you, my dear girl, and I will be coming to bring you back to my home because there's no place in heaven for someone like you.

The white world that once was has now turned to black.

The solid ground has split and cracked and crumbled apart. She looks at the buildings around her—this is the place she grew up, the city of her youth, the home she was going to make with Dan for possibly the rest of their lives—and everything is broken and falling apart. Everything is gone.

All the grass and so many trees—burned to the ground from the fire and the hail coming from the heavens.

I will survive and I will take you with me sweet child of mine.

The voice talking sounds friendly and familiar but it breathes cold air behind her ear and inside her soul.

She finds herself on the edge of a crimson sea with dead forms floating and washing up on shore. The charred remains of ships float on the water like drifting coffins.

This will pass just like it did when God wiped us all out with the Flood.

Skylar stands on a black hillside and sees a stream of water flowing over her bare feet. The water isn't clear but the same color as the ocean. The same color as the dead on the streets and in the buildings, the same color as the blood on the cross.

That's not real it was never real and you don't have to keep thinking about it.

The voice is coming for her, waiting for her, wanting her. It has wanted her all her life and it's finally going to take her to a place she can't leave. A place where she'll spend eternity. A place full of fear. A place full of pain.

The skies darken and the sun dims. But men and

women around her continue to suffer from the heat and the air and the sun breathing fire on their skin.

"Make it stop," she begs God.

But it's too late. Too late to ask for another chance. Too late to make the judgments stop.

The locusts come again, but this time they're not tiny but huge, hulking beasts emerging out of the pit to reign with terror.

Come to me, my child, take my hand and let me lead you to a place where you won't have questions.

But she fights. Skylar clenches hands that burn and opens eyes that wince and holds on to a hope.

"Please, God, please," she cries out.

But this dream and nightmare and horror are all real. This is not a movie and it's not a story and it's not a sign of things to come. It's arrived. Her life is like the lone fish in the dark ocean of blood and she's barely hanging on.

"Help me," she says as liquid fills her mouth and her lungs and she coughs up the blood.

The beasts are coming to get them. Coming to kill more. Coming to do as much damage as they can before their fate is once and for all sealed by their Maker, the one they turned their backs on, the one they chose to revolt against.

War has arrived and the world is now paying for its sins.

For *all* their sins.

37
CONFESSIONS

They find a kitchen with a fridge and an oven and a sink in it. The only thing it doesn't seem to have is anything to eat. Tommy goes through some of the cupboards but finds them empty except for paper cups and plates.

"So where are your parents?" Tommy asks Sam while still looking.

"Killed. Or taken. Whatever they're calling it."

Tommy eventually spots a lone jar of peanut butter. He tosses it to her. Sam catches it without looking surprised.

"Hope you don't mind crunchy," he says.

For a second she studies the jar, then laughs.

"I don't want to add anaphylactic shock to our day. I'm allergic."

She tosses it back to Tommy. He nods and places it on the counter so he can dig into it later. It'll be his second jar of the day.

There are some cans of different types of fruits in the next cabinet. He picks out a can of peaches and tosses it her way, then begins looking for some kind of utensil. "Here, I got a spoon for you."

As he brings it over to her, Tommy sees she can't open the can. He takes it from her and pops off the top. She thanks him and quickly takes a bite.

"Bet you're hungry," he says.

"I haven't even thought about food until now," she says with a full mouth. "But yeah. I'm sorta starving."

He considers what she said about her parents, then wonders if his are gone too. All he wants to do is head back up to Chicago to see if they're there. To see if they survived.

A part of him believes they're still there. But that's just a hunch.

"So you believe that this is the Rapture?" he asks Sam.

"That's what everyone is saying."

"Not everyone."

She takes another bite and remains silent. Tommy realizes his reply probably sounded a bit biting, a bit aggressive.

"I don't know my Bible that well but I just have a hard time thinking this is something that came straight out of it," he says.

"I don't know."

"That's just it. I don't think anybody knows. You see all those people out there? You think any of them know?"

"But isn't that because . . ." She pauses for a moment. "Because they're the unbelievers?"

Tommy shakes his head. He has no idea and it's frustrating not knowing. Not being able to do anything. Not being able to have any sort of comeback or witty statement on any of this.

"So why are you still here?" he asks her. "You're obviously a good person."

Sam finishes the jar of peaches. "I *am* a good person. Just not a *churchy* good person."

"You never went?"

"In case you hadn't noticed, I'm not really a sit-in-the-pew sorta girl. I don't like rules." She thinks for a moment. "Guess I blew that one."

He notices the look on her face. "Yeah, guess I blew that one too."

They stand in silence as Tommy notices his camera sitting on the kitchen counter. "I always hear people saying, 'Where was God?' when this or that happened," he says. "Do people really think God could do all of this to the world? Do you?"

"He destroyed the world with the Flood. Right? Noah and his family and the animals were the only ones left."

"That's a kids' story," Tommy says.

"Not quite. Not when most of the world dies. Does *this* feel like a kids' story?"

“It feels like I’m in a horror movie.”

This doesn’t make her smile, though he’s not exactly trying for any kind of laughter anymore. He’s just being honest.

“I think I’m past the point of looking for some kind of scientific explanation or something,” Tommy says. “But God and judgments and believing and not believing. It all just feels so made-up and so . . . so corny. The burning buildings and the dead people out there—that’s real. But even now—where’s God? Where is he? That still doesn’t seem real. And I just . . . I don’t know if it ever will be.”

He sees her giving him a strange look. “What?” Tommy asks.

“Are you this comforting all the time?”

He smiles. “Nah. Just when the world’s ending.”

Maybe it’s seeing the video of the ocean receding and the dead sea life strewn all over its shores that’s making him want to start filming again. Or maybe it’s what he filmed half an hour ago with Sam and the words he uttered while looking into the camera. The spark to the fire inside doesn’t really matter. What matters is that it’s time to continue the job he was supposed to do today. There’s a reason he was asked to start filming and there’s a reason he’s going to keep doing it.

The world needs to know.

The world . . . or at least some of the people in the world.

Maybe some of the few remaining souls left in this world.

Enough's enough, Tommy decides. He can sit around waiting and wondering and eating peanut butter all night or he can go ahead and do something.

Leaving the peanut butter on the counter, he goes out to find his friends. He wants to film them again, to hear from them, to get their thoughts. This is the something he's going to do. He's going to ask some questions and capture some moments.

He finds Allison and Jack in the room next to the triage. "How's Skylar?"

"She's still out," Allison says. "Dan hasn't left her side since coming back. She's been having some terrible dreams. Mumbling about weird things. Blood and dead fish and all sorts of weird stuff."

"I want to get you guys talking to the camera, okay?"

"Now?"

Tommy nods, turning the camera on. "Something we can show our children one day."

Neither of them like his joke, but he doesn't know what else to tell them.

"Come on—what do you want to say to the camera?" he asks Allison.

"I don't know," she says. "Like a confession?"

After everything that has happened—the chaos in the streets and the long night waiting and Skylar being sick and all of them being stranded here—Allison still looks beautiful. She's beautiful inside and out and always will be.

And I'm glad you're still here. So very glad.

"Sure," Tommy tells her. "Get something off your chest. It feels good."

"I don't have anything to confess."

Of course you don't.

Allison looks over at Jack, so Tommy follows that gaze with his camera.

Your turn, buddy.

"Anything you want to say, Jack?"

"Yeah. Why are you still filming?"

"If we don't make it out of this, someone needs to know what happened to us."

Jack doesn't like that comment and makes a face at Tommy. "Don't even say that. We're gonna make it."

Tommy keeps the camera pointed at him.

"What do I say?"

"I don't know. Whatever you're feeling."

Jack sits up for a minute, nods, looks directly at the camera, clears his throat. "Fine. My name's Jack Turner. I don't know why this is happening—but it's not gonna beat me. I'm not ready to call it quits so I'm not sure why you are getting us to do last-minute confessionals."

"Do you love Allison?"

Jack pauses for a moment. He can't believe Tommy just asked that. Neither can Allison.

But I did and there. It's out there. Time for some resolution. Time for something, at least.

"Of course," Jack says, smiling and giving Tommy a shrug.

"It's taken you seven years to figure that out?"

"What?"

Jack seems to be in disbelief—confused and annoyed and also a bit embarrassed.

Good.

"I just want to know how you feel," Tommy says.

Jack shakes his head, looks at Allison. Tommy can see the shocked look on Allison's face.

"Tommy, what are you doing?" she asks.

"I almost lost her tonight," Jack says in an angry and defensive tone. "How do you think that feels?"

"So it takes almost losing her to feel something? That's not love, Jack."

Jack curses. "What's wrong with you, man?"

Tommy is still holding the camera, still looking at them and still demanding to know. It's a loaded weapon he's holding, full of questioning ammunition.

"I just think she deserves someone who really loves her. She's a great girl. It's been seven years. . . ."

Jack stands up, looking like he's ready to pounce on Tommy. He's more than annoyed. He looks furious. "You know what I think? I think you have a confession you need to make, Tommy."

"I don't have one," Tommy says.

"Just say it. Say it!"

"Say what?"

Allison is standing and starting to move between the guys.

"You spend all your time with Allie. You don't date."

"Stop this, guys!" Allison shouts.

"Say it!"

A hand reaches and grabs Tommy's camera, then aims it back at him. He's not sure if Jack is going to film him or bash him on the head with the camera. Tommy tries to move out of the frame but Jack pushes him back, forcing him to be filmed.

Suddenly Tommy decides that if he's going to be filmed, he might as well make the most of it. The only audience he ever wanted and dreamed about is watching and listening. He looks at the camera, then at Allison, then at the camera again and back at her.

"I love you, Allison." *There. I said it. I confessed. It's done.*

"I knew it!" Jack seems more triumphant than furious.

"You're saying this . . . now?" Allison asks. "Now, Tommy?"

"I'm sorry."

"What am I supposed to say to that?" she asks.

"I'm really sorry. All those times—I never had the courage to tell you even though I wanted to."

That's enough for Jack. He drops the camera and lunges at Tommy, slamming him to the floor and wrestling with him. Jack doesn't punch him like Tommy might've expected. But he grabs at his throat and Tommy is forced to hold him off in a stalemate for a few moments while Allison tries to intervene.

"Stop it, guys!" Allison begs them.

Suddenly a voice ends the conversation. Not in a loud, booming curse but in a soft reflection. They all stop and look and see Dan at the doorway mumbling something.

It's Skylar. Something's happened. She's gone.

Tommy listens and waits for the worst.

What he hears instead shocks him. It shocks all of them.

38
ALL APOLOGIES

"It's easy talking to you."

"I just like asking questions."

"You like listening to them too."

"Yeah, I guess."

"Jack doesn't have the patience to listen to my rambling thoughts. They drive him crazy."

"He's already crazy. You can't be driven to a place you're already at."

"You're a bit crazy too. It makes sense with your friends."

"Does it make sense you're dating him, Allie?"

"I don't know. Sometimes nothing in this world makes sense. I sorta came to that conclusion when my parents

divorced. I thought they were meant to be together. They were all I'd ever known about love and marriage and all that. And one day—it was gone. One day I blinked and it was no longer there."

This distant memory surfaces in Allison's mind as she separates Tommy and Jack. Only hours ago she assumed she had lost them. But now, in some weird way, she fears she is losing them again.

Skylar unconscious. Dan sick with worry. Tommy and Jack wrestling around with one another and their anger. And Lauren already gone.

The group is disintegrating in front of her very eyes. And for the moment, in this church in the dark shadow of what used to be Wilmington, North Carolina, Allison wonders if she's breaking apart too. Or if they're just all pieces strewn about on the floor waiting to be picked up. Waiting to be put back together.

Waiting with no hope of any answer.

But a strange voice silences Tommy and Jack's fury.

"Katie Murphy."

Dan says this in a tone so faint and dark that they almost don't even hear it. But they do, especially Tommy, who says, "Dan" in a way that's warning him to stop.

Behind Dan, Skylar lies there, no longer in her wedding dress, no longer conscious. Dan's face wrinkles up with frustration and anger.

"You guys want a confession? Here's one," Dan says. "It was after the LSU/Alabama game. I gave Katie a ride home. It was just that moment—we both got caught up in it and without thinking. It happened. We had sex. We did it."

Allison has no idea where this is coming from and only hopes Skylar isn't listening.

Why in the world is he saying this now? Just like Tommy and his terrible timing.

"You and Sky were taking time apart," Tommy says. "It wasn't cheating. We talked about this."

It didn't count.

But they all seem to know and realize that yes, it *does* count. It will always count.

"I tried to tell Sky before we got married. When we went to counseling. When we were supposed to tell each other everything, when we were supposed to not hold anything back. She deserved the truth—she still does."

"It doesn't matter now," Allison says. "Stop talking."

If anything will push Skylar further into her black fog, this will be it. So just shut up, Dan. Don't try to control the issue like you control so many other things except Skylar, the one person more controlling than you.

Dan shakes his head at her, his face so earnest. "Everything matters now. Don't you see that? I'm a liar. In every way."

The new groom looks down at his new bride with a gaze that's both loving and sad. He brushes her blonde locks away from her face, then gives her a gentle kiss on the cheek.

"I'm sorry," he tells her softly. "I'm sorry I waited until now to tell you, Sky."

Jack is standing and brushing himself off as he shakes his head and curses.

"So, Tommy. Confession time was a great idea. What did we learn from this? Huh? You're an idiot."

Jack leaves them and heads out of the room. Normally Allison would follow, but not this time. She looks at Tommy, not angry at him but just confused. Then she goes over and sits beside Skylar.

She can't take any more confessing. By anyone.

39
THIS IS NOT A TEST

Men don't share their emotions. This is one of the things Tommy's father tried to teach him, though Tommy has always tried to steer clear of being like his father. But the older he's become, the more he's realized that he can't help it. It's part of his DNA to be and act like Don Covington. So Tommy's naturally drifted toward being someone who hasn't shared a lot and hasn't dug too deep.

But today and tonight are all different.

Tommy enters the kitchen looking for Jack. Thankfully he finds his friend sitting there drinking a cup of coffee. He slowly walks over and then points to a chair nearby. Jack nods, so Tommy sits.

Tommy takes a deep breath, then begins to share something he normally would have tried to bury down deep.

"Look, you know I love you like a brother. During these last seven years when you haven't been able to pull the trigger, Allie and I cultivated a friendship. I was her go-to guy to help her try to figure you out. She would cry on my shoulder about you. Over time, I started getting powerful feelings for her. I fell in love with her, Jack."

He's about to continue but a woman enters the room and opens the fridge. Tommy lets her grab a bottle of water and smile at them then depart before he continues.

"I'm so sorry, Jack. I literally said, 'Please, please not this. Not her. Anyone else but her.' It's been seven years of misery for me. Carrying this around, not saying a word. I know you love her—of course I know that."

He just wants to hear that it's okay, that it's all right. That *they're* all right. He wants Jack to give his laid-back "That's cool, man" and then have him say let's just forget about everything else. But Jack doesn't do this.

He's not doing a thing.

Which is understandable considering everything.

Tommy rubs his hands together. They feel sweaty.

"I just wanted to say sorry. That's all."

There's more to say. A lot more. But Tommy doesn't have the words. And Jack probably doesn't want to hear them anyway. He sure looks like he doesn't want to hear them.

I just want to go find a mattress like the kind Skylar's sleeping on and drift off and not think of any of this.

"I get it," Jack finally says.

Tommy nods. It's enough for now. Tommy stands and leaves Jack by himself. There'll be more time to talk later. Now he just needs to figure out their next step of action.

Tommy stops at the doorway and looks in to check on Skylar. She's pale, like a child with a deadly illness. She shivers, yet sweat soaks the mattress that Dan and Sam stand next to. Then Tommy hears someone singing.

It's Sam.

She sings a soft melody, something that sounds like a lullaby. He doesn't recognize it, but it doesn't matter. It sounds like something real and something sweet, something from the days before the dark came. It sounds like life. It almost makes him cry because everything in the last ten hours or more has been so dark and dreary.

Sam sings and tries to comfort the sick bride on her deathbed.

Soon the song ends and the darkness seeps back in. Tommy hears Dan asking the nurse about the wound, then watches as she checks it.

They all can see the obvious. The wound is worse. It's horribly infected with grisly black veins that spiderweb out. The puncture wound doesn't just look black. It looks charred over like the skin of a hideous burn victim.

Dan covers his face as tears come. Tommy puts an arm around his friend.

"There's nothing I can do," Rachel tells them.

And that's all. There's no hopeful *but* that comes. *But wait until the medicine kicks in. But wait until the doc comes by. But wait until we send her into ICU.*

There are no more buts *that are ever going to come. We butted ourselves out of a civilization by being harmless and careless and soulless.*

Soon another song begins. But this one doesn't seem to bring as much hope as the other one. This one only seems to haunt.

Tommy leaves the room, having seen enough misery for the moment.

Misery, however, awaits in other places. In seemingly every place Tommy can step into.

It's amazing what fear and despair and anger and confusion can taste like, how they can feel like they're shifting around in the body. Tommy has never felt more alive than this moment, but he knows that's maybe because death is so close. He's never felt so cold inside his gut because of the angry fire burning all around him. He's never felt many of these emotions and it's an awesome and terrifying thing.

There's a larger room that was probably used for Sunday school, though that's all Tommy's imagination offers for most of the rooms. *This room? Sunday school. This one? Um, another Sunday school. Oh, and the one with all the kids' stuff? Nursery.*

They've got a television on and some of the survivors are watching a channel. There's an actual channel playing. It can't be cable or anything like that. Maybe it's like they did in the old days with televisions that picked up signals from the air with those weird antennas. The screen is hazy but they can see enough. They don't want to see what the screen is showing, not really, but they look on like witnesses to the world's great car crash.

Tommy looks with them.

People running on a street. Terrified. Shuffling around like animals, like ants. Some carry suitcases and bags. Some trip and get trampled. Others stand on the side of the street screaming at other people or themselves or whoever. The faces have fear and panic and confusion all over them, the same feelings Tommy and everybody else have inside their souls.

Total and complete chaos.

A voice begins to talk.

"International reports are coming in from Lagos to Cape Town. St. Petersburg is the latest to confirm that churches are being attacked."

They see an image of a building burning. Probably a church. Then another, this obviously a church with its towering steeple.

Why the churches? Why?

"There's a local relief center staged at the Cape Fear Bridge, and rescue teams are bringing in food and supplies—"

The screen scrambles and flickers on and off. Then there's just static from the speakers as the emergency broadcast symbol appears on the screen. Tommy has never seen it before except in comedy sketches or movies. But turning the channels, that's all they see. The same emergency tone and symbol on each channel. And a message that seems to tell them they're all doomed.

"This is the Emergency Broadcast System. This is not a test. Emergency services are temporarily unavailable."

Everybody in the room just watches, not saying a word, surely thinking the worst just like Tommy is.

Tommy doesn't want to see any more. But his mind can't shut off the voices inside.

This is the Emergency Broadcast Soul. This is not a test. Your life is basically over and you also just told the love of your life how absolutely crazy you are about her. And you haven't seen her since. So yeah. The end is here and you're forever a total loser, Tommy. Loserrrrrrrrr.

Tommy looks around the room and suddenly notices a couple in the corner, cuddled and asleep.

It's Allison and Jack.

This is the Emergency Broadcast Psyche. This is not a test. She chose Jack. Perhaps you need to choose the river or the great big devil monsters outside or something—anything better than this scene.

He just wants to get out of this room, but before he does, Sam stops him.

"My biology teacher told me that by stimulating a part of the brain with electrodes you can make a person fall in love with a rock," she says with a friendly smile. "I bet they have some electrodes lying around here somewhere."

Tommy nods. He likes this girl. He's glad she was stubborn enough to stay by their side and get this far.

40
WAKE-UP CALLS

The day burns, the crowds thick, the drinks overflowing.

I never want this day to end. These days. These friends. These moments.

I want to be twentysomething my whole life. Not worried about the future or about finances or about my ultimate fate. God and family and my fortune can be put on hold for the moment. Just so I can listen to music and drink beer and laugh and talk about my favorite reality show and what I just tweeted about.

Every day is a hashtag waiting to happen. The biggest question is which one.

What's going to be the next hilarious video to find on YouTube?

What's going to be the next sort of fun outing with the gang?

How can I spend my check fast enough?

It's not about next year or next month; it's about now. These songs, these feelings, these moments.

Nothing else matters and I sometimes wonder if it ever will.

Time. Oh, if Tommy could only have a little of it back.

Time is not their friend now. It seems to wait like a rabid animal crouching in the darkness.

Tommy can't sit still, so he heads out to the lobby in the back of the church where he can pace and think about what they should and shouldn't be doing. Soon he's joined by Jack and Dan. The three guys back together again.

Well, Mr. and Mrs. Chapman. Here's the church you two wanted for Skylar.

The thought is twisted but so is every single thing Tommy can see. Dan looks like Skylar has already died while Jack remains his intense, silent self. Sam joins the group but doesn't say anything. This is one of those times when talking is way overrated and unnecessary. There's nothing to say except the obvious.

The one to break their silence is Rachel.

"The antibiotics aren't working," she tells Dan.

Dan seems to already know this but still looks stunned and heartbroken. "What do you mean?"

"The infection's spreading," the nurse says. "It's acting like a venom."

Tommy looks at Jack and Dan. Just that word freaks all of them out.

"You thought she needed antibiotics. Now you're saying you're not sure?"

"I've never seen anything like this. She needs an anti-venom like Anascorp or at least a doctor who can help. I'm sorry."

"Do you think anybody out there in the church is a doctor?" Tommy asks.

"I tried. I asked everybody."

"I'm taking her to the hospital," Dan declares and starts walking away until Tommy grabs him.

"Wait a minute."

Tommy knows Dan's ready to do anything, including die. The look on his face confirms it.

Dan jerks his arm to get free of Tommy. "It's just on the other side of the freeway," Dan tells him. "We'll make it."

They stare at each other, Dan not about to back down.

"The other side of the freeway?" Tommy asks. "We almost didn't make it thirty feet."

"I'm not saying it's a good plan—but it's the only plan that'll save Sky."

"It's only a couple of hours until dawn," Jack says in an exasperated, tired tone.

"What's that got to do with anything?"

Tommy realizes what Jack's talking about.

"Those things—they have only attacked at night. Whatever they are, maybe they're nocturnal."

Dan thinks about it and seems to understand that maybe they're right.

"Does Skylar even have a couple more hours?" he asks the nurse.

She nods. "I'd wait till morning."

The nurse soon leaves them, wanting to go back and keep watch over Skylar. Dan finally agrees to wait—for the moment.

"We leave for the hospital the second the sun comes up. Got it?"

Tommy's never seen Dan so decisive and so reckless. But he's never seen Jack want to rip his head off, nor has he ever seen Allison so withdrawn.

They're already dying, all of them, in their own little, awful ways.

The restlessness drives Tommy back toward some of the meeting rooms. He finds Pastor Shay in a small room just off the sanctuary, watching old news footage on his tablet. It almost appears as if the pastor is trying to hide out in here. Tears line the man's face and he appears deeply moved. Or deeply disturbed. Or maybe both. Whatever Shay is watching, it's prompting a profound reaction. That's all Tommy knows. He walks inside and takes a seat to watch the footage with the man.

The news, now hours old, is awful. The world is being wiped away slowly but surely, like the notes on a dry-erase board being rubbed off bit by bit. Tommy doesn't cry like the pastor but he does feel sadness and fear. He just doesn't know what to do with them. Crying isn't going to change anything.

The pastor shuffles in his seat and leaves the tablet on a chair beside him while he folds his hands and closes his eyes. Tommy expects him to say something, but there's only silence. The muffled audio from the news report is the only thing he can hear for the next few moments.

When the pastor opens his eyes, he looks at Tommy. "That's the first real prayer I've ever said. Do you know how powerful it feels?"

"Can't say that I do," Tommy admits.

"It's not too late for us to believe, you know. God still loves us. I know that. I believe that, now more than ever."

"And if I do—if we do—we'll get out of this mess? We'll be raptured?"

"No," Pastor Shay says. "The Rapture's over. We missed that boat."

Maybe there are some airplanes that can come down? Or can we simply take a car?

"That's not good," Tommy says.

His tone is overly sarcastic, but the pastor's not biting. There's nothing remotely funny to the pastor about any of this.

"It isn't," Shay tells him, "but we have hope in this path

to the Father and in his gift of eternal life. You have to make a choice, Tommy."

You're sure sounding like a preacher man now.

Shay stands up.

"What are you going to do?"

Considering the look on the pastor's face, Tommy thinks he might do anything. Who knows. Maybe the guy will carry him over and baptize him right here and now. Tommy's not sure how that all works. But the fact that this somber, scruffy-looking guy actually happens to be a preacher is a surprise to begin with. So anything he might do won't be too unbelievable.

The pastor has a sad-looking smile on his face. It reeks of regret. "I'm going to be a pastor for the first time in my life."

More people have come into the sanctuary. Some stand around the perimeter and in the back. Others sit in the pews, waiting for some kind of hopeful word. The lights are dim but still work overhead. The faces looking around at one another seem heavy and overcast and scared. Conversations are hushed. Smiles are abandoned. Everybody is feeling and thinking the same thing yet nobody wants to utter it out loud.

That changes when the pastor walks to the front and asks everybody if he can have their attention. "I want to share a few words with all of you," Pastor Shay tells them as he stands on the platform at the front of the church.

Tommy scans the room and finds Allison and Jack sitting near the back in a pew. He takes a seat beside them but doesn't say a word.

The pastor stands there holding his Bible, a stoic look on his face. Tommy can tell the man is trying to hold back his emotions.

"For those of you I haven't met, I'm Pastor Shay."

He pauses for a minute, looking around, clenching his jaw.

"I have been a fraud. It's true. I walked into this church years ago—ten years ago, in fact. I became employed with an occupation and that is what I did. I merely occupied. I walked through this sanctuary with my soul asleep. But I'm not sleeping anymore."

Everybody in the room listens with full ears. Not one head is turned away.

"In Matthew, Jesus said there will be those who use his name, give fancy speeches and sermons, but he will turn to them eventually and say, 'I never knew you.' And I was one of these people. I was a charlatan—a traveling salesman passing through life. Hocking God's wares. Something miraculous had to happen to open my eyes to the truth of Jesus Christ. I hold myself responsible for not only my failed faith, but everyone who counted on me yet still stands here today."

"What can we do to save ourselves?" a voice calls out from the crowd.

The pastor looks to the ground for the moment, then

back at all of them. "Those of us gathered here—this is our wake-up call. A kick in the pants. Oh boy did we ever get one."

Tommy looks for a moment at Allison, then at Jack. He wonders what they're thinking.

I have no idea what to think so I'll reserve that for now.

"Our path will not be easy and will not go unchallenged. This is our opportunity. I can *now* show you the way. We can share this journey together."

As the pastor speaks, Tommy can hear a slight fluttering. That soon becomes louder and louder. A flapping, a thumping. Violent. Soon the noises become loud and aggressive thumps and seem to be hovering somewhere outside the church.

More of those things, those monsters, the demons.

"Did you hear that?" Tommy whispers to his friends.

Pastor Shay stops. There are audible gasps and concerned voices sounding off. The flying, flapping sounds continue.

Then the lights go off.

Someone screams.

Tommy stands up, making sure Jack is at his side.

Lights flicker and the flying creatures are still outside making loud noises and landing on the roof and shaking the building somehow.

This can all go away these creatures don't have to hurt us.

The people in the church are rushing out of the pews, slamming into each other, yelling and cursing and crying.

"Let's get out of the main room," Tommy tells them.

They head to the entrance of the church. Faint light spills on all of them. Voices are asking what those things are and what's happening. Somewhere back in the sanctuary, Pastor Shay is still standing, still waiting to continue his speech.

Somehow the thing outside senses when they are near the front door. Or the things—who knows how many there are. There's a scratching sound, like sharp knives scraping the other side of the door. It sounds so loud, so close. Tommy can almost feel them on his skin.

Jack slowly moves people away from the door. All eyes are on it now. Even the pastor, who walks into the entryway, is staring at it.

"Move to the back of the church," Jack calls out.

He's close by Allison, almost making sure he's protecting her. The group of people move away from the door. Some are totally freaking out. Tommy tries to calm them as he moves with them. He hears someone calling out his name.

Sam.

He keeps walking but the voice shouts his name louder. Tommy turns around and gets nudged and then nearly knocked over by people frantically trying to seek safety.

Nobody cares anymore. It's just about me me me.

"I'm coming," Tommy shouts out to Sam.

The things are outside, scratching and clawing to get in. They're on the sides of the church now and the front door and the roof and everywhere.

How many are there?

He finds the white-haired punk girl and grabs her hand tightly. "Don't let go."

They both run to the back of the church now, Tommy trying to find where Jack and Allison went. It's madness. One minute the pastor is talking about Jesus and wake-up calls and now there are things trying to rip off the walls and doors surrounding them in order to get inside.

The roof sounds like it's about to either come off or collapse. Tommy hears the pastor's hoarse voice shouting at them to get to the basement.

Yeah, go to where we're burying the dead. That way we won't have to carry your bodies very far.

A woman stumbles and falls and people simply run over her. Tommy helps her up while keeping his hand clenched onto Sam's.

It's total chaos in here. Jack is helping lead the group downstairs, opening the basement door at the top of the steps and ushering people in. Tommy nods at his friend as he passes, following Sam into the darkness below.

Who knows what awaits them down there?

41
RUINER

The lights flicker like fireflies in the night until they finally go out, leaving the group in darkness in the cold, musty air of the basement. Jack slams the door shut and now they're down here in relative silence, in the unfinished open area with the graves of the dead nearby.

Tommy turns on the night vision in his camera and sees Dan cradling Skylar. The faces that look into the camera are ghosts and zombies counting the seconds before they're finally free of this nightmare.

But there's only one way for that to happen.

Tommy doesn't know some of these people. Most, in fact. Yet they're all down here huddled together in fear and in darkness. He's videoing them in order to keep this for whoever comes next. For whoever's left. Assuming he's gone.

Unless, of course, we're all gone.

"Where's Rachel?" the faint voice belonging to Skylar asks.

It wasn't long ago that she was saying how much she loved Dan, how much she adored him and how she couldn't wait for their future. The promises and the dancing and the wine and the fun.

Tommy shoves the thought away.

This is all we have now and this is all I can do.

"Rachel?" Tommy asks out loud.

He looks at everybody his camera is picking up but doesn't find the nurse anywhere. Then he hears the sounds again. The fluttering beat coming, a heavy and ominous pounding.

The sound comes from above the church but they can hear it even down here.

There are some cries and gasps.

The thrashing continues like some loud, angry animal punching the walls and the rooftop.

The camera wavers as Tommy's hand shakes. There's no sign of the nurse.

"Rachel?" he calls out again. "Has anyone seen Rachel?"

"The nurse? She was in the triage." It's a woman in the shadowed crowd talking.

Tommy shuts his eyes for a moment and curses to himself.

"Rachel's out there," Skylar says in a weak voice. "We have to—"

Someone screams. Not like a scared-you sort of scream but a painful, hurting scream that continues for a while. Getting closer. And closer.

Jack opens the door a crack. Tommy looks out and can hear the scream approaching.

No no no.

It's her. She's racing to get down the stairs.

But something wants her it's taking her it's grabbing her.

Jack starts to move but Tommy jumps on his back and prevents him from going out there and being a moron.

A dying moron.

"Jack, no, come on."

Rachel falls and climbs to her feet again but then something—some dark shadowy hand—swoops in and takes her and slams her against the wall, her lifeless body suddenly a kid's doll bashed against the hard, flat surface with malice. Tommy pulls Jack in.

The door slams shut.

The silence is sickening.

Tommy pictures Rachel's body being bashed back and forth and doesn't know what could do such a thing. What kind of demon can pick you up and flail you around like that? What kind of things are they dealing with?

The hushed cries all around him are the answers. Nobody knows. Nobody knows and one by one they keep dying. Violently and unexpectedly and suddenly.

As Tommy and Jack stand a few feet away from the locked door, Pastor Shay comes and puts his head by it.

Something is behind it. Something breathing. Something sick, waiting and wanting all of us.

The scratching starts. As if it can smell the pastor and knows who's standing there and wants to rip the heart and soul from this man. It sounds like a dog wanting to get in. Not a little dog but a feverish devil dog clawing with its two front paws, ripping into the door until the thin barrier can't take any more.

The pastor and Jack lean against the door. It looks like it's about to pop out, to split or be crushed. The rest of the survivors are moving away from the doorway.

Faint, heavy, sickly whispers can be heard outside.

Skreeeeeee

Scratching, hovering, pushing, tapping. They want inside. They want them. They're hungry and they're not going away.

"Listen to me," the pastor calls out to Jack and Tommy. "Get everyone out of the church—after—"

More scratching, frantic and panting and breathless.

Then a thunderous bang comes. They can all feel it and it shakes them.

No.

Tommy's eyes burn and his gut clenches without breathing and without looking. Every loud thud or pounding or scrape results in someone screaming or whimpering.

"What are you going to—?" Tommy starts to say to the pastor.

"Just listen to me!"

Another loud boom.

They're coming. They're going to break through.

The pastor begins talking in a hoarse, frantic voice but one with full authority. "There's a relief center set up outside the city, at the Cape Fear Bridge. They have supplies. Get everyone out of the city."

"What are you talking about?" Jack asks, still pushing back on the door that's buckling and popping.

"We know they're attacking the churches, these things. Get these people to the relief center. And whatever you do, stick together."

Tommy puts his camera down for a moment. He thinks he knows what's about to happen.

That can't happen he's not going to do it he's not crazy.

"What are you doing?" Jack asks.

"There is only one way out."

It's not going to end this way. No.

The loud bang startles all of them, including Tommy, who ducks for a moment since it seems so close. And then before he can do anything or say anything, the pastor moves to the door. Then he looks at Tommy.

"I've seen it in you," the pastor tells them. "Lead them out of here. You can do it."

The pastor opens the door a sliver.

"They're here for me," he tells them.

Then he shoves Jack away from the door and opens it all the way.

"I'm so sorry."

The words . . .

Who'd he say them to? Jack? Me? All of us?

But Tommy doesn't think so.

They were for the God he supposedly followed and served and preached about for his whole time as a pastor. The words were directed upward.

Pastor Shay steps through the doorway and then opens up his arms and the hellish creatures smother and snap and suck the man's body. The bones crack and buckle under the demons' grip as the pastor begins to howl in a way Tommy's never heard before. Shay's body is lifted and snapped and then seized into the darkness all while his bloody wails continue.

Tommy and Jack both slam the door shut and soon the bellowing stops. They wait for a moment. Then something massive slams against the door. It sounds exactly the way a one-hundred-and-eighty-pound dead body would sound hurled up against a door.

The corpse of the pastor is just outside. The something seems to snatch it up again and slide it away.

Then . . . silence. Strange, eerie, awful silence.

But the monsters are gone. For now.

42
BREATHE

Breathe. In. Out. Again. Once more. In. Out. And again.

These are the simple thoughts running through Allison's mind.

Breathe. And again. And again.

Sitting on the hard cement, the part of the basement that isn't dirt, Allison covers her legs with her arms and waits and listens. She can't sleep or even begin to. She keeps waiting for the clawing and scraping to start again.

The unholy, hellish sounds don't resume.

It doesn't keep her from shivering with fear.

We were just all dancing together listening to rap and rapping along with it.

Time doesn't care about them anymore. And God? Does God care?

Are You up there? Are You watching? Can You even hear me with all the other carnage You have to deal with?

Her heart wants to just stop. Her eyes want to roll back in her head and stay there.

The world ended. *Ended.* Ended right in front of her face. And still it rips apart, bit by bit. A pastor sucked up and snapped and spit back out by something. Something she can't even speculate on. What can do that? Who can do that? And who can *allow* that to happen?

If this is Judgment Day, then she has lots to pay for. For not being a good girl and not believing and not caring and not submitting.

I'm a big, fat, failing sinner and I'm going to die soon.

She knows this.

Allison knows this and it hurts to breathe.

The world is over and I might as well be over and it comes down to this thing this whole big bad thing I do or don't believe in.

Thoughts swirl. End-of-the-world stories aren't supposed to be like this. They're supposed to have ways out. They're supposed to have sweet moments of grace. They're supposed to have sweeping orchestral music and A-list actors and bright lights and rainbows all coming at the right moment to bring salvation.

But none of those things are happening. None of those things are coming.

It's just silent and dark and lonely.

Breathe in. Breathe out.

She tells herself again. And again. Huddled and hunkered down and hungry and utterly and completely flying off the handle.

God can You hear me please God?

Please.

In.

Out.

43
THE DAY THE WORLD WENT AWAY

Where are You, God? Where are the tiny strands of light in this dark place?

Where is the sunset? Have You forgotten to turn it on? Have You finally let us put out the fire?

Can You only hear me if I'm on my knees, with my hands folded, with my eyes closed?

Do I need to be afraid?

Do I need to be fearful?

When will this night be over or will it ever?

When can I wake up and see the normalcy we all once had?

I want it back. I want to rewind the video of life. I want to redo. I want to redo it all.

But does that mean I have to accept You're behind it all?

The cracks in the door allow streaks of sunlight to cut through the darkness they've been huddled together in all night. Tommy is cold and sore and exhausted yet his mind still races. He wants to get out of this hole, to get away from the dead bodies buried not so far away, to feel the sun on his face and breathe in fresh air. He also wants to try to do something, anything, to fight the creatures that are attacking them.

We have to be able to do something, right?

Jack is the first out of the group to stand and move to the door. "I haven't heard anything for a while," he tells them.

"Don't do it," someone says.

"Maybe they're gone," another voice says.

The discussion continues as Jack ignores it like always and does his own thing. He opens the door a few inches, and dust floats in the air as more light makes Tommy squint. No screams. No demon sounds. Nothing yet.

"I think it's okay," Jack tells them.

Tommy stands and looks over to Allison and Dan and Skylar. Several times in the night, he heard Skylar's haggard breathing and her soft moans of pain. She's made it this far, however. There's hope for her.

There's hope for all of us. The sun brings that.

They begin to file into the hallway and then climb upstairs around the debris of broken windows and cracked walls. Jack has to push open the door leading to the sanctuary. When Tommy follows him, he can't believe what he's seeing.

There is something hypnotic and beautiful in the carnage that awaits them. The holes in the roof and walls of the church allow streaks of sunlight to crisscross throughout the shadows of the church. The pews are overturned and littered with glass and wood and plaster. What remains of the stained-glass windows have been melted from the outside, as if someone placed a blowtorch right next to them.

Jack turns to them with horror on his face. "Don't look up there," he says.

But Tommy glances at the front of the church and sees the body of Pastor Shay hanging upside down over the altar. Blood drips from his unrecognizable face. He resembles a garbage bag that was tossed and didn't quite make the can. Nearby, the leather cover of the pastor's Bible can be seen. Jack steps over it and kicks it, spilling out pages that are now simply ash. Tommy is reminded of what happened to Skylar's Bible after she was attacked.

The banner that hung on the wall with a Bible verse on it now is simply bits of cloth with words that have been shredded into the dust floating around them.

"Come on, let's go," Jack tells them.

Nobody says anything but continues walking. Not

long ago the lifeless man hanging over the altar spoke to them about faith and hope. Now they pass him by like the wreckage in this room. Something broken and disposable that they're leaving behind.

A loud crash makes everybody jump. Tommy shields Allison from the sound, then realizes it was only a light fixture plummeting to the ground.

It's going to be nice to get out of here and breathe air that doesn't have the stench of death connected to it.

The group of survivors begins heading down the street in the direction of the bridge where the relief center is supposed to be. Tommy is torn between wanting to follow Pastor Shay's instruction to lead them and his loyalty to his friends. In the end his friends win out, and the broken bridal party from Dan and Skylar's wedding just stand and watch the others slowly disappear. The sun is up above and the clouds are gone. It actually feels like a normal day—if, of course, you were to forget about all the dead bodies and wreckage surrounding them.

Skylar struggles to hang on to Dan's and Jack's shoulders for support. She barely made it out of the church. What's going to happen on their trek to the hospital?

"The hospital is just across the freeway," Dan says. "There's gotta be a doctor there or medicine."

"We need to go with the others to the relief center," Jack says. "Shay told us to stick together."

"They've probably got medical supplies there," Allison adds.

"No. Rachel said she needs an antivenom. We're going to the hospital." Dan doesn't just sound determined. He sounds like an angry, possessed man on a mission.

"Don't worry about me," Skylar says in a voice Tommy can barely hear.

Tommy takes Skylar for a moment while Dan and Jack continue to talk about what to do. Allison seems to have had it with her violet dress that's already scraped and frayed at the bottom. She starts to rip it to shorten it and allow her to walk better.

Glancing at Skylar, Tommy can see the shrunken cheeks and the loss of color. Everything that was bright and beautiful about Skylar twenty-four hours ago seems to be gone. She's a shell that's slowly starting to crack and dry up.

She's not going to be alive much longer.

"We can make it to the relief center," Jack says.

"I'm not taking that chance. Skylar needs help now."

Two alpha males competing with each other when they really need to be working hand in hand.

"Doesn't the word *relief* spell help to you?" Jack asks.

Dan looks red-faced and unlikely to budge. "You have no idea if there really is a relief center. We know there's a hospital. We know there's doctors and medicine there."

Dan takes Skylar back from Tommy and starts to guide her in the direction of the hospital, but Jack blocks his way.

"Get out of my way," Dan tells him.

"No."

"Skylar's dying right here. Do you understand that? I can't lose her. She's my wife."

"I'm not letting anyone else get hurt. Now let's get going—"

Dan immediately lets go of Skylar and rushes toward Jack and the two of them fall to the ground. Dan doesn't know how to fight, so the scene is darkly comical as he tries to secure a choke hold on Jack's neck but gets nowhere. Jack pops him in the head but doesn't want to fight his friend.

Tommy makes sure Skylar sits on the grass before intervening. He gets between his two friends and curses and shoves both of them away from each other. "Knock it off. Both of you. Dan's right. We have to try the hospital. I'll go with him. We'll meet you at the relief center. Okay?"

Jack looks at all of them. "No. We stay together. We'll all go."

Allison looks sick, like she's going to cry again.

Tommy nods at her. "It's going to be okay. We find medicine and then we'll be on our way to the relief center."

Sam is nearby, waiting to see what happens.

"You good with that?" Tommy asks her.

"I'm okay," Sam says.

"Let's get moving."

Every passing stranger either ignores them or stays away, scared of their group or maybe just slightly out of their mind as they should be. Everything around them carries scars, as if some giant wiped a mighty claw over everything and left shards and slivers behind. Streets are cracked, the cement crushed and fragmented. Buildings are half there, ransacked and abandoned and mostly reduced to rubble. Vehicles litter everything, from parking lots to grassy lawns to intersections. Everything is cluttered and discombobulated. Yet actual living, breathing souls are seldom seen.

Maybe they're all dead and everyone left has gone to the relief center.

The sun bears down and Tommy sweats and feels a little more like his old self. This is his daily workout like he used to always have. Now all he has to do is go back to his apartment and back to his old routine and his old life. But those are all gone.

Strange images come to his mind.

The watch he had hoped to save up for all year to finally buy. The one he didn't really need because who really actually looks at a watch for the time anymore anyway. The one that seems ridiculous now since he might as well be counting down the minutes and seconds himself since the end is not near, it's here and it's now.

The job he didn't get that gave him sleepless nights. The worry and the angst and the frustration. Like the watch, so meaningless.

Then there's the woman walking in front of him, the one walking in step with Jack. The girl he's been in love with for a while, the one whom he finally told the truth to. The big revelation, only to result in a whole lot of nothing.

You spend long moments worrying and wondering only to see them wash up on the shore of a sea of wasted hours. Only to see them stranded on the island of foolishness. He wants that time back. He wants that energy back.

I want everything back. I want to redo so much I have no idea where to even start.

He wipes his brow. Unbuttons his cuffs and rolls up his sleeves.

They pass by a helicopter that's on its side and split in half. It's just another thing to notice and then leave behind.

As they enter the shadows underneath the freeway ramp, Allison asks the question all of them are thinking.

"What if nobody's at the hospital?"

"Someone will be there," Dan says as he continues to assist Skylar in their walk.

Allie glances back at Tommy. He gives her the best smile he can muster.

It's not much, but it's all he can offer her right now.

44
IN THIS TWILIGHT

We sit and watch the sun start to nod off to sleep. Side by side on this swing, a small dog on my lap. The snug feelings of being overfed and overcomfortable and overloved. Holding his hand in mine. Just . . . being.

A small house. Fixed up to perfection.

A small lawn. Nothing too much.

Small things to decorate the small tree of our life together.

Small because we don't need much. We just need each other.

That's all anybody needs, right?

Right?

Allison knows that was the dream once. This thing she held on to even after growing up and realizing that the small house with the picket fence doesn't really exist. Yet still she has saved it for herself.

Now, watching the weary world all around her, Allison knows the picket fences are forever gone. The whitewashed house on the corner with the little white dog and the white cabinets is a blinding mirage in a hot, searing desert. Nothing will ever be whitewashed again. Nothing.

Come to me, child.

She finally spots the entrance of the hospital, but all she can see is people leaving it. Cars and SUVs and ambulances litter the parking lot and the lawn. She notices a dead body that's surely rotting in the hot sun strapped to a gurney right next to the ambulance it must have been carried in.

Dan leads Skylar and the rest of them to the entrance. The sliding-glass doors are jammed open.

"Think those things that attacked us are gone?" Sam asks.

"They must be," Tommy says.

Dan turns to them. "Let's hope there are still some doctors here or something."

But it's obvious once they walk inside that it's going to be a long shot.

The reception area is empty. The place looks like everything else in this new world: ransacked and messy and overturned and out of sorts. Chairs are tossed on their sides. Bodies litter the floor. Glass covers the ground. The electricity is out, the lobby illuminated only by the sunlight.

Dan is now carrying Skylar in his arms. "Let's find her a room and lay her down."

They begin walking down a hallway that only gets darker the farther they get from the entrance. A pharmacy on their left is bare, its shelves picked clean. Some empty bottles are on the floor along with upside-down furniture. Jack jumps over the counter and begins to look through everything but there's nothing to find.

We made a mistake coming here.

As they look for a room, they see a woman dressed in a nurse's outfit helping a patient out.

"Please—we need help. Anything you can do."

The woman doesn't listen to Dan's plea. "There's no one left. We're getting out. They've got supplies at the Cape Fear Bridge."

The nurse continues to walk with her patient.

Everybody is leaving.

We should've done the same.

More bodies litter the floor and the rooms they pass. So many dead. So many lives just taken.

And so many left behind in total and complete despair.

Dan soon finds a room with light coming in through the windows. He gently places Skylar in the bed while Jack and Tommy look for any kind of medicine that might help her.

Allison pulls up a chair beside the bed, stroking Skylar's hair and trying to get some kind of response. But none comes.

Tommy heads into another room but soon comes back and slams the door shut. "Looks like there's nothing left."

"I'll go floor to floor," Jack says with a voice that sounds slightly out of breath. "Find her a doctor, something to help her."

They've gone from one prison to another.

Allison holds Skylar's lifeless hand. "You're going to be okay, Sky."

"We're going to beat this," Jack says.

But Allison knows the reality is that there's nothing to beat. The game is over and the victor has been chosen. They're merely spectators in the crowd trying to figure out how to get back home after watching the war unfold.

Jack heads out of the room. Tommy waits for a moment, then tells them all to stay there. But before he can leave, Allison tells him to wait a moment. She stands and goes over to the doorway.

"You're right, you know," she says.

Tommy just looks at her, confused.

"The first night we met. I still remember it too. You're right—we did just click."

She gives him a hug and whispers to him to be careful. He gives her a caring, gentle smile. Then he's gone.

Allison knows it might be the last time she ever sees Tommy. Or Jack. Or both.

Sometimes there is so much grief and terror that the well inside starts to overflow. And it's all you can do to keep your head above water to breathe. There's no thinking and no planning. There is just doing. You just keep doing what you need to do.

And right now, what Allison needs to do is be there for Skylar. To help her dying friend before it's too late.

Allison and Sam sit against the wall watching the couple in the shadows. Dan can only hold Skylar's unresponsive arm in his hands and watch her. The three of them—Dan, Allison, and Sam—are quiet while they wait for the guys to come back with any kind of hope. The formerly glowing bride is now pale and bloody and unconscious. They all know it's just a matter of time.

"I read somewhere that the light you see when you die is the brain releasing massive amounts of endorphins to ease the pain of death," Sam says.

"There are a lot of people who think that, but there are a lot of other people who think the light is a sign of God's existence," Allison replies.

"Do you believe that?"

She nods, thinking of the prayer she prayed this morning in the darkness of the church basement. Crying out for help and salvation in the pit. Asking, begging God to help them and save them. But no help or salvation came.

But I still know God's up there. He has to be.

"I do. If these bad things exist out there, then surely there are good things. It all depends on how you look at it."

She feels something stirring inside her soul. The ticking

clock, the kind that's winding down just like Skylar's life, can almost be heard. It's following her like the violent fluttering of the demons.

Allison knows there's unfinished business between God and her. She just still doesn't know what to say. Or how to say it. Or when to say everything.

How do you finally come before your Maker after a life of running away from him?

45
DARKNESS

It can feel and taste their fears, their anger, their questions. It also can see the bright light that tries to break these things. It's attracted to that light to blot it out.

There is the fighter named Jack, the doer. The one always leading, the one always ahead even though he doesn't know where the path leads. He currently looks through empty drawers in empty rooms but it knows he will find nothing but the very thing residing in his heart and soul. Emptiness.

Jack is with the other doer, the more reserved soul who watches and waits, the one named Tommy. The two of them continue room to room looking for hope, looking for answers, looking for salvation. They pass the chaplain's office and see the chaplain dead at his desk.

The dead don't speak and don't give answers because they're long gone. Just like these two will be soon enough.

They arrive at the cafeteria and Tommy asks Jack if he can smell the odor in the air. They open the door to find the stacks of bodies. Rotting, decaying bodies in a hot, dark hospital.

It knows this is the end. This is the time for it and its kind to finally do anything and everything they want. To wreak havoc. To cause chaos.

It gets closer, watching, waiting.

"Do you hear anything?" Tommy asks.

It can see his fear, his frustrated soul that wants to do something but can't. The anger. Oh, the anger in these two. Anger at the one who caused this. Anger at their Maker, the one they refuse to even acknowledge.

It knows its Maker and knows its God and knows the pecking order. It knows where it will be eventually. But all it can do now is continue to hurt and harm and cause this kind of exquisite terror.

"Shh!" Jack says.

It watches them in the dark. They can't see it but it can see them. Can feel them. It puts a hand so close as if to touch them. But not now. Soon but not now.

The farther they get, the more terrified the two young men become. It delights knowing the slight sounds it makes result in this. Good. That's what it wants.

Soon there will be other business to attend to as well.

"Come on," Jack says. "Let's keep looking."

They look, not knowing it follows them. It's been trailing them for quite some time.

It's waiting until it's time.

It's waiting until it can finally end their hopes once and for all.

46
GONE

The two figures argue even while they die. They argue about the man between them. This man who didn't do anything to be with them. This man who still hasn't said a single bad thing about anyone.

Dying.

And one of them condemns the man in the middle, mocking him, ridiculing him, demanding something. Anything.

But the other calls the ridiculing man a fool.

"Don't you fear God even though you're about to die?"

This is what the man tells the other.

"We deserve to be on these crosses but this man doesn't. He's innocent."

Then he tells the dying man in the middle the only words he can utter.

"Jesus, remember me when you come into your Kingdom."

In between the darkness and the light, Skylar remembers this picture. This scene. It unfolds as if she were standing in front of the three hanging men on their crosses. She hears the words and knows she wants to be like the second thief. She wants to believe. She wants forgiveness.

Please Jesus . . . remember me. Please . . .

Then her eyes open and she sees Dan smiling at her. Skylar knows it's almost time to go. Each breath is a strain. She can't move, can barely speak, can barely even see.

But I can believe. I can do that.

Poor Dan. Poor Dan.

"Hi, sweetie," she barely manages to get out.

"Sky, I'm here. I'm here."

Allison and Sam approach the bed as well. They seem to be in disbelief that she's still coherent.

"Are you hurting?" Dan asks.

I've been hurting my entire life in one way or another but no more.

"I don't feel anything," she utters.

"That's good."

He brushes her hair. She knows Dan would have been a good husband. He would have been there for her at all times. He would have provided for them. He would have been a good father. She smiles at him, and in response Dan starts to cry. She doesn't want him in any more pain.

"Dan?" she whispers.

"I'm still here."

She thinks of the crosses, of the man in the middle. This person who was very much a man, this man who could very much die. A God who allowed him to do just that.

God's Son.

It's unbelievable and always has been.

Until now.

"If you didn't go to church where I grew up, people looked at you funny. You know that. It was a thing—maybe a Southern thing. So that's what I did. But I never really believed. I never really, truly thought there was a Jesus who came down to save me. I never really understood that I had all these sins that needed forgiving. But I get it now. I get it and I want you to know—it's okay. I forgive you because God forgives me."

Dan looks at her. "How did—?"

"I heard you tell the others," she says. "We all make mistakes. There's a place we can take those to. There's a thing we can nail them to."

Her eyes close for a moment and she sees the cross in the shadows of the fading light.

"You can nail it to the cross and let it go, Dan. You can let someone else take that burden."

She breathes out. She's scared. Yes, scared and uncertain.

But the peace inside her soul balances that. She ties that peace around her heart.

"I can see it now," she tells them. "It's . . . beautiful. It's so . . . bright."

It's the bright light of sandy, warm shores and morning sunlight and reflecting snow and shining stars. It's glorious. She sees it all and it welcomes her with a glowing smile.

"She can't breathe," Dan says.

His voice echoes from far away.

I need to leave you.

"Stay with me," he calls out. "Please—Sky—stay with me. Please."

The restlessness. The confusion. The never-ending intensities. The fears. The longing. The desperate, needy, selfish longing for more.

It's all gone now.

"Please. No!"

With all the strength she has left, she squeezes his hand.

Death is not about despair. It's not about disappearing. It's about finally knowing and declaring that there is a heaven and an eternity.

It's not too late, Dan. It's never too late.

She feels like the thief who slipped in just in time.

She feels joy.

She finally feels free.

47
HOPING AND PRAYING

"Why?"

The voice scratches across Allison's heart like grinding fingernails on a chalkboard. She stands staring at Dan and the distress on his face. Not even twenty-four hours ago, the same face stared at the girl of his dreams and pledged to be there for her in sickness and health till death separated them. But death isn't supposed to be here. Not so soon. Not now.

"Breathe with me," Dan yells to the empty body. "Someone help me."

She puts a hand on his arm. "There's no one here to help her."

Dan keeps trying, holding Skylar, not giving up.

"Breathe." Between sobs. "Breathe."

He soon sees that she's nothing more than a corpse. Tears run down Dan's cheeks as he shakes his head in disbelief and anger. "No."

She sees him clench his fist and his jaw.

Still shaking his head, he looks toward the window. "I hate You!" he shouts.

Allison doesn't ask whom the comment is directed toward. She's thought the same things, but that's only because it's too late.

It's too late for all of them.

In the darkness, still clinging to the faint hope that they can save their friend, Tommy and Jack look through another room. Jack is searching a closet when he stops for a moment and turns to Tommy.

"Why do you have to get to a point where something's going to be taken from you to realize how important it is?"

Tommy nods. He doesn't know.

"It's sad," Jack continues. "That it had to take the end of the world for me to wake up."

"You don't have to explain. I know you love her."

Jack stares at him for a minute. There's no anger on his face. Just exhaustion and bewilderment.

"Thanks for being there for her."

"Don't screw it up," Tommy says, breaking the serious mood with a little levity.

They both laugh. They're okay. They're cool again.

Neither of them knows that things are far from cool back in the hospital room they'd left. Things have gone from bad to worse.

And things are only going to continue downward.

Allison sits on her knees by the bed holding the body of her closest friend. She closes her eyes to pray but can only see Skylar's smile and Lauren's big, bright eyes. Laughing as they walked, the three of them, hand in hand on the beach. The sun hovering in the sky, the future staring at them with a smile. So many plans talked about. So many dreams shared.

All gone. Forever gone.

She knows her parents are gone. The rest of her family. Whatever friends weren't at the wedding. All gone. All dead. All taken by God.

But I was left behind. I didn't deserve to be taken.

So she silently prays. There's nothing left to do. She can weep for Skylar or she can curse God or she can sit there dumbfounded but she chooses to ask—no, beg—for forgiveness. For another chance. For hope. For grace.

God I'm sorry I never thought of You.

For nearly three decades, Allison has only thought of herself. Of her plans and her career. Her love for Jack and her place in the world with him. Her friends. Her things. Her, her, her.

Please God help me. Help us all.

She knows she deserves to be down here with the rest of the remaining souls. Those who didn't bother to find time or energy or care to have a real relationship with God. Who never thought anything of his Son and who never really even believed in his Spirit.

I know You're the only way, God. Please. Please help me. I want to believe. I want to see the light. I want to know there's still hope and still time. Wash away all my mistakes like the cold creek water rinsing muddy feet. Make me clean, Lord. Make me Yours.

Dan curses behind her. Her body shakes and the tears lining her cheeks won't stop.

I ask that You save me, God. I believe in You and believe that Your Son can take away my sins. Please, God. Please, Jesus. Please.

"What are you saying to the Man Upstairs?" Sam asks behind her.

Allison turns and stands, seeing the Goth girl looking at her with skepticism. "Apologizing for what it took for me to realize the truth. Hoping he's taking Sky into his arms right now. Hoping—praying—that there's room to take me as well."

Dan paces the room and curses as he listens to her words. "How can you sit there and pray to a God that would let this happen? Seriously, she was your friend."

"Dan—"

But he storms out and leaves them.

Allison understands. She could be angry. She *is* angry. But she has no right to be angry at God for supposedly abandoning them when they've spent their lives abandoning him.

She sighs. Then has an idea.

There's not much time left.

She knows the clock is ticking and there's just not enough time to say the things that need to be said.

"Will you do something for me?" Allison asks as she picks up Sam's phone.

Sam nods and looks curious.

"It won't take long," Allison tells her. "But it's important. Life-or-death important."

48
ALLISON

I want more than a simple statement that I believe. I want to belong to someone.

I want to stop trying to rationalize my existence away. I want a relationship.

I want to hear something and have it bring some life to this soulless, meaningless world we live in.

I want a Spirit that doesn't fail me or flunk me or frustrate me but rather fills me.

I want to experience the feeling of being on my knees and knowing the meaning. Of falling before my Maker and knowing and realizing that he wants me and he desires me and he really, truly loves me.

God loves me.

God is waiting. For me.

I know this now and all I want is to finally be at peace.

49
FORSAKEN AND FORGOTTEN

And so it comes. The rush. The fall. The breakdown.

Another empty, ransacked room.

Another dead end.

Tommy feels something and stops for a moment, looking around the white hospital room with an empty bed and even emptier cabinets.

"Do you hear that?" he asks Jack.

It's obvious that the screaming is coming from outside. Jack and Tommy hear the voice and instantly they recognize it. They rush to the window and tear at the cheap miniblinds.

Dan . . .

He's outside on the lawn of the hospital. Screaming and shouting at the sky. Waving his fist.

"I hate You! You hear me?"

Tommy can hear him fine and knows if there's a God above he can hear Dan too. Not that he'll pay any attention. Not that he'll care.

But others will. Others like those weird winged devil creatures out there.

"No," Tommy says.

"Stop!" Jack screams at him through the glass. "Be quiet!"

Dan falls to his knees. They can see he's crying. Screaming and spitting out his words. Furious.

Skylar's dead.

Tommy knows that.

But where are Allison and Sam?

Dan is depleted, destroyed.

"Do You hear me?" he shouts. "Do You? Are You even listening to me? I'm right here. Come on."

But he just kneels there, this lone figure on the grass in his tux pants and stained white, tattered shirt resembling what his heart must feel like.

Tommy and Jack continue to scream at Dan but he doesn't hear them or doesn't care.

Much like God must be toward Dan's complaints.

Then Dan's angry face turns to something else. Sorrow.

"Please, God. Just take me."

Dan cries and mumbles some more words that Tommy can't hear.

"Oh no," Tommy says.

Everything about Dan suddenly changes.

The anger subsides.

The wrathful look turns to a look of peace.

Dan is mumbling something under his breath.

He's asking God to save him. To forgive him. The whole thing.

They continue to pound against the window. Dan needs to get off the lawn and back in the hospital. He needs to get out of clear view of anybody and anything.

No no no this is not how salvation comes not like this not this way.

A breath. Then Dan turns and sees them for a moment.

No please God no not—

Then something sharp and long and curved slices through Dan's chest, spewing blood all over the white of his shirt. His body is crushed against the lawn.

The guys scream.

The creature hovers above Dan, giant, sickly, coiled, black-gray, and grotesque.

Dan's face hangs just above the grass, his mouth spilling blood, his eyes lifeless, his heart and soul gone.

Screaming doesn't help. Pounding on the windows doesn't help.

The thing—the hovering huge beast—whips back up into the sky and takes Dan with it.

Tommy bends over and wants to cry and wants to throw up.

Dan.

Gone.

Skylar.

Surely gone.

Leaving Allison and Sam.

"We have to get back down there to the girls," Tommy says.

Jack is not with him anymore. He's there but he's gone. Just like Tommy feels. Just like everything.

"Come on, Jack," he says. "Come on. We don't have much time."

They don't have much of anything left.

Allison.

She can still be saved and they can still get out of here and find whatever kind of relief is left in this godforsaken, God-forgotten place.

Running.

The hospital a cemetery full of sleeping zombies.

The halls deserted shadowlands.

A trip and a fall and back up again.

Everything blurry. Everything heightened and messy and broken.

Tommy turns and takes the stairs two at a time.

He remembers everything.

All the laughter and the smiles and the late nights and the talks and the dancing and the drinking and the dreaming. So much joy. So many moments. Stuck now in a place just like this. Empty rooms full of empty cabinets. Ransacked and stolen and taken away. Chipped, fractured, pulverized, destroyed.

Everything filling his mind and his heart, not going away and not leaving him.

It'll be with him forever.

However long forever might be.

The body in the bed is the first thing Tommy sees. It doesn't move and doesn't look good. He touches Skylar and knows for certain.

"She's gone, man," he calls out to a breathless Jack. "She's gone."

Jack is next to him.

It's too much it's way too much and there's more there can't be more right there shouldn't be.

"Where are the girls?" Jack asks.

"Maybe they went to look for us?"

Please yes.

"Allie!" Jack's beginning to lose his voice from all the screaming. Yet he continues to call out her name.

"We have to find them," Tommy says.

He doesn't want to leave Skylar here alone in this room, but he knows they need to leave the dead in order to find the living.

They head to the front of the hospital, where the

sliding-glass door is still slightly open and broken. The dead bodies are just like window dressing now. It's odd how you can get used to things so quickly in this life. The overturned chairs and the papers and the empty supplies on the floor and . . .

What is that?

Next to a broken mirror is a phone.

It's Sam's phone.

Tommy breathes in. Surely this can't get worse. Right?

"No, please no, no, no."

Surely they're outside waiting on them.

Surely. Yes, right. Surely?

Jack is down the other hallway and calls out, "She's not here. Allie's not here."

For the first time since everything started, Tommy feels defeated. He picks up the phone but he knows. He already knows.

His fearful heart feels something new.

It feels crushed like the glass he's stepping on.

He sees the phone in his shivering hand. Then slowly he turns it on to see what it might reveal.

But Tommy already knows and is already prepared.

He shuts his eyes for a moment.

50
HOPELESS PRAYERS

His fingers open up the playback app on the smartphone and find the video that waits there. Tommy pushes Play.

It's Allison, running, the phone jerking from side to side as Sam runs beside her, the ground flashing by beneath them, the cries and screams of the girls, the sounds behind them. Awful sounds, scurrying steps following, following, until there's a thud. The camera slamming to the ground.

Suddenly the camera is turning and then stays put only to show a blur and a figure in violet being shaken and then thrown into a wall behind a counter.

Tommy has no more air inside him. He feels like choking but can't breathe.

"What did you see?" Jack says behind him. "Where are they? What's wrong?"

Tommy scans the room without saying anything. Then he sees the cracked wall and the torn debris around the counter. He goes over there with Jack following.

Allison's body is mangled in the corner beneath the crushed wall she landed on. Streaks of blood line her face and her arms and her dress.

Jack vaults over the counter and goes to her side but then hesitates. It's almost as if he's afraid to touch her.

He kneels and begins to wail, screaming out her name.

Tommy just stands there in an almost dreamlike stupor. "Allison," he says in disbelief. "This doesn't make sense."

He goes over to hug both Jack and Allison but Jack fends him off with a curse and violent reaction. "Get away from her," Jack shouts. "I should have never left."

Tommy slumps to the floor as he watches Jack blubber, not wiping away his tears. It's a striking, haunting thing, this full-of-life, full-of-answers jock becoming a whimpering mess whispering to his dead girlfriend.

Dead.

Dead.

Tommy fights his own tears by doing something. By moving. By searching the room.

Sam was with her.

He knows she's gotta be somewhere.

"Sam's not here," Tommy says. "She must have run or something. We have to find her."

Jack is cradling Allison's broken and bloody body. His tears fall off his face onto hers. Tommy doesn't know where to go. He doesn't want to leave Jack, not like this. He's afraid of what his friend might do.

There's a sound behind him and Tommy turns, fearing the worst.

Then he suspects something else.

"Sam?"

He moves toward the overturned reception desk.

"Sam, is that you?"

Sure enough, the girl is huddled behind the desk, her eyes closed, her body shivering. When he touches her she looks and then jumps up and latches onto him with a fierce hold.

"I hid—I was hiding—it didn't get me—it was chasing us—I was so scared—that thing—where's Allie?"

"You're okay now."

Sam's questioning look. Jack holding Allie's body. Dan speared by some *thing*. Skylar dead and left alone.

It's too much.

Too much.

Tommy leans on the desk and begins to cry. His thoughts race and hurtle and rush over each other.

He's got a prayer he wants to pray.

God do You want me then You come find me and take me. Do it and take me and take everything You can because I'm not going to just lie down and let You do it easily.

Come on.

Come on can You hear me?

Sam's hand is on his shoulder as his tears burn his eyes and mess up his cheeks.

Do You see me do You hear me do You know how tired I am of hearing of You?

I'm not a bad guy.

I'm not a mean soul.

I've done some good things and some bad so what do You want?

Why did You leave us all?

Why did You even bother?

What sort of thing are You trying to tell me?

Tommy wipes his eyes and then covers his face with wet hands.

Yeah I'm alone and yeah I'm terrified is that what You want me to say?

Do You want me to admit that You're there? That I'm afraid? That I acknowledge You doing all of this every little bit?

What more?

Your Son and Your Spirit and all of that stuff I haven't heard about since leaving Sunday school?

I don't know anything more. I'm tired and I'm weak but I'm not going to just give up.

He looks at a distraught Sam, who stares at him and looks afraid. Then he glances over at Jack.

Come find me, God.

Come grab me.

If You want me then come and crush me down like You've

done with the rest of this insignificant world. Like You've done with everyone close to me.

Crush my body and soul.

Do it and end this all.

Of course, nothing happens. Tommy gets control of himself. He knows they need relief. Physical and mental and emotional and every kind of relief they can find.

"We have to go," he tells them in a restrained voice.

"No," Jack shouts back. "I'm not leaving her."

Jack is as delusional and upset as Tommy.

"Jack," Tommy says, "you're my best friend and you know I won't leave you. But we do need to leave. Now, let's go."

"I'm not leaving her again! Just get out of here."

Tommy stands his ground. "No."

He climbs over the counter and tries to help Jack stand up. But his friend only shoves him away.

"Leave us alone," Jack shouts. "I mean it."

Tommy keeps trying. "She's gone, man," he tells Jack.

But Jack doesn't want to hear it and needs to lash out. He stands and attacks Tommy, sending them both to the ground as he begins to punch Tommy's head. Tommy covers his face to defend against the blows, and Sam comes over and tries to stop them. She pulls Jack off Tommy.

"There's nothing else out there that I want," Jack says,

more tears cutting down his cheeks. "Nothing. I'm staying with her."

"Then I'm staying too."

Tommy crawls over the counter and collapses into a chair.

For a few minutes there's just silence. Then Jack moves over the counter and walks toward the entrance. "Let's go," he tells them.

Tommy doesn't hesitate. He simply follows his friend outside with Sam walking next to him.

There doesn't have to be an explanation. Not in this hell, this madness. Nothing makes sense. Nothing.

Jack lost himself but he's back. For the moment. He's back to trying to battle and beat this thing.

Tommy's battling too.

As they step outside in the fading light of day, Tommy looks up to the sky, wondering if God heard his prayer.

Wondering if God cares.

51
HOW TO DISAPPEAR COMPLETELY

"You think we'll be hanging around ten years from now?"

Dan's question is unusually melancholy but it's because he's unusually drunk. It's the night of his bachelor getaway and we're looking out over the shimmering skyline of Vegas.

"Absolutely," Jack says.

He's had his share tonight too.

"Dan's gonna get married and then Jack will and I'll be forced to come to Vegas all by myself." Yeah I guess I've had a little too much too.

"Dan won't be able to come," Jack says. "Skylar won't let him."

"Jack won't be married," Dan replies. "He'll be working here."

"What about me?"

They laugh at my comment.

"Good luck to whoever marries you," Jack says.

"That's not nice."

"You're too much of a thinker. You're gonna kill your wife with questions."

I can only laugh at Jack's unusually honest comment. "Yeah, maybe. But what about you? You're never gonna settle down long enough to even have a wife."

We spend a half hour joking around like this until Dan becomes serious. "I'm gonna miss you guys."

"We're not going anywhere, are we, Tommy?"

"You're stuck with us the rest of your life," I tell him.

"The rest of your life," Jack says in an ominous tone.

And it was true. Dan was stuck with Jack and Tommy. They just didn't know the rest of Dan's life would be so short.

They didn't know a lot of things.

Memories sneak up and find Tommy. Strange memories. Lots of them. He can't shake them the same way he can't move too quickly. He and Jack and Sam are exhausted and confused and careful.

The sun fades. But at least it's still hanging up in the sky. At least there's that.

The sights are still there for their small group to see. A dead body hanging on to the edge of a car door, as if it were about ready to get out of the vehicle when boom. The big thing happened and the body was just left.

The streets are all abandoned. They don't pass any moving souls. Everything is empty, broken, desolate.

This isn't the dream people always told Tommy about. The whole thing about growing up and growing older. About pursuing your dreams and passions once you've gotten your diploma and left college. Finding the right work and the right woman and the right winning plan for your life. This whole end-of-the-world scenario really doesn't fit into the plans. They never told him about this.

Nobody once uttered a single word about it.

Tommy walks and sees everything gone.

This isn't happening.

But he is still here and this *is* happening.

The smoke swirling all around him is making the fading sky even more black-and-whited-out. Bodies can be seen. The dead watch sightlessly from the street, from cars, from corners, rotting away like trash from a McDonald's.

I'm not here.

But his legs are moving and aching. His back and neck and forehead are sweaty. His mouth is dry and thirsty. His heart is empty and depleted like his bank account used to be in his college days when he'd drink his cash away. He wishes he could go back and have one more rowdy night. One more raucous outing with his friends. But they are mostly gone now.

I'm not here.

That Tommy—that smiling guy so smug and so smart, the one videoing his friends' wedding—that guy is gone. Forever gone. In his place is this angry, self-serving, surviving soul.

But me and my video recorder are still here. That's right. Still here.

The world drains out and starts to get dizzy and delirious. But he keeps them moving. They keep moving.

Maybe there's hope ahead. A fire pit in the dark. A smile in the blackness.

He turns and sees Sam, the white-haired Goth he initially wrote off. She's got fight left in her. And that's good. She'll need that.

They will all need that.

Who knows what tonight and tomorrow will bring. It surely won't be anything good.

Soon the sun is gone and darkness hovers around them. And hope—whatever tiny morsel of it might have hidden deep inside Tommy—now seems long gone like the sunshine.

Ominous, unnatural clouds have started to form in the skies. Seeming to follow them. To shadow their trek through the city, whatever remains of Wilmington.

"Are we going to the Cape Fear Bridge?" Sam asks while they walk.

"Yeah," Tommy says. "Once we get there, we should be okay."

Tommy notices Sam playing around with her phone.

"There's something important I want you to see," she says.

Jack is still leading the way, several yards in front of them, not talking or looking or worrying about them.

"Let's get to the bridge first," Tommy says.

They move along a street, then cut down a flight of stairs leading to the riverfront. They can see a trash can burning on the walkway with several survivors standing around it. Nobody looks at them and they don't stop to talk.

They climb another stairway back up to the road and soon find themselves walking in the middle of an off-ramp. A car in the distance is burning. They hear noises near the car and then can hear a fight taking place. A group of men are stomping all over some poor soul.

Tommy and Jack rush over to help. The orange and red streaks of fire light their way but it's hard to see what's happening and who's who.

A gunshot fires and the group of men disperse. Tommy finds Jack on the ground. His head is bleeding from one of the men bashing him with something. Tommy helps Jack get up and together they rush back over to where Sam's standing, trying to stay safe.

The other man stands up, the one who was being beaten, and manages to raise the sign he was carrying.

Tommy reads it.

Repent—The Day Of Reckoning Is Here!

Tommy is about to offer the man some help when his eyes become large and he shouts out, "Repent!" as blood drips from his mouth.

Insanity. Everything is completely insane.

They leave the man behind as they keep moving.

Soon they can see the Cape Fear Bridge and the relief center just beneath it.

"There it is," Tommy says.

"It's really there," Sam says.

Jack is holding his bloodied head and isn't walking as fast as before. Tommy knows they need to get to the relief center.

Then maybe everything will be okay. Even for just a short while.

52 CHOICES

Spotlights illuminate the base of the bridge. There are hundreds, even thousands of people moving around, filing into the wharf where tents are set up and vehicles are parked. There are ambulances and semis that are open with supplies in them. Hundreds of cars are crowded around the area, but there are avenues open to the relief workers.

Tommy, Jack, and Sam are moving with the crowd. They see generators working and power—sweet, glorious electricity lighting up this area and providing hope. Providing life.

A nurse stops them and tends Jack's head wound, cleaning it up and bandaging it for a temporary fix. She tells them to keep moving down the wharf, where there's food and other supplies.

"I thought there wasn't going to be a relief center," Sam says. "I thought it was too good to be true."

Tommy nods and agrees with her.

Me too.

Anything that offers a little light and hope seems too good to be true anymore.

The crowd murmurs and sounds a little more lifelike the farther they walk. Someone mentions that they've brought in chaplains. Tommy's not sure what that means. He thinks of Pastor Shay, how he finally believed, and how he also volunteered to give himself up.

What a wonderful thing to do. But then again, the pastor believed he was going to a wonderful place.

A place where his family waited.

Tommy used to think it was a wonderful world. Like the song. He remembers hearing it at the wedding during one of the slow dances. He used to see skies of blue and clouds of white. But nothing is blessed and sacred anymore. Nothing is wonderful and barely anything is left of this world.

He pictures his friends and how they celebrated right before the end. How they smiled and laughed and danced and cheered a new love. A new day. A new life.

But they're gone now.

The roar of helicopters sounds above their heads as they pass by relief tents to find one that might have room in it for them. It feels like there's a war going on and they're finding shelter after being on the battlefront.

So what side are you on?

The words knock on his heart, working on his soul.

Where are you going and what are you going to do when you get there?

The questions haunt and prick and hurt.

If this is the end why are you still running so fast so far?

The words beat like drums and he breathes in and tries not to have to answer.

Tommy is still here. Still breathing. Still able to move. Still able to battle back.

He doesn't plan to stop at any point. Yet the darkness sweeping overhead and the dim shadows sucking up his soul make everything so bleak and black and bitter.

They finally reach a tent where they find blankets and food. The smell of vegetable soup fills the air. People sit around, eating, resting, surviving.

It's temporary hope, but for now, it's glorious.

For fifteen minutes, the three of them sit with blankets around them while eating cups of hot soup and drinking bottled water. Such simple things—things to bring them warmth and comfort—aren't taken for granted. Tommy knows the soup in the Styrofoam cup might be the best cup of soup he's ever had. Ever.

People keep filing in and finding rest around them.

Stories can be heard of the same nightmares over and over again. Most seem too tired to manage anything more than a whisper. There's a hushed sense of doom hovering over everybody.

"How's your head?" Sam asks Jack.

"It's fine."

"Yeah, you always were hardheaded," Tommy says.

"Please don't give any speeches at my funeral," Jack says with a wry smile.

"I won't because that's not going to be happening for a long time."

Jack gives him a nod for the little bit of encouragement.

Once they've finished their soup Sam digs out her phone.

"I need you guys to see something." It's the video she tried to show Tommy earlier.

She wiggles between Jack and Tommy and presses Play.

There, on the screen, is Allison.

Beautiful, vibrant Allison, the woman both of the guys watching love. The one in the strapless violet dress and the messy dark hair.

You still looked beautiful even after the world ended.

Tommy knows a part of him doesn't want to see this. He should just get up and walk away. It'd be better that way. Whatever Allison might be saying is something that might possibly haunt him for the rest of his life. However many years or months or days or hours he has. He thinks this, yet he stays still and silent.

"I need to tell you guys something," Allison says, speaking directly at the phone. "And I'm saying this now because I'm afraid—I'm afraid there might not be another chance to do this."

She seems nervous as she takes a breath and steadies herself.

"I was wrong. I realize that now. I've spent my whole life telling myself I was spiritual and that was enough. Obviously that didn't work out too well. But now I've found real faith. I made a real commitment. These demons—they are trying to remove the Word of God from what's left of the world."

Tears fall down Allison's cheeks yet she continues to stare at them and continues talking.

She was always strong. Always.

"Don't you see? It has to be the truth—even they recognize it. God's words are the only thing that can save us. That's why they have to destroy them. And they want to destroy us too if God's Word is in us. It's their biggest threat. And once we know the truth . . ."

She wipes a hand across her face to get rid of the tears.

"We all have a choice. We either choose to accept and believe and get life like we've never known it, or we choose to live our lives selfishly, ignoring God, and end up dying anyway."

There's a slight sound fluttering in the background. Allison turns her head around, a startled look on her face.

"We don't have much time left on this earth," she says in a hurried voice. "You have to make a decision."

Now it's a loud thumping that can be heard. She looks around again.

She knows.

She knows she's about to die. Yet she's still talking. She's still making sure we hear what she has to say.

"I choose God," Allison says. "What do you choose?"

She closes her eyes, knowing what's next. Knowing and accepting and feeling strong enough to do so.

Tommy takes the phone and turns it off. He's seen enough.

Seen enough. Heard enough. Gone through enough.

He doesn't even hear Jack get up until he notices his friend standing along the side of the tent talking to a chaplain. They're engrossed in some kind of serious discussion.

"She wanted you guys to see that," Sam says.

"She always cared about others," Tommy says. "Even to the very end, that's what she was worried about. Us."

"I'm sorry."

"I'm sorry I wasted so much time," Tommy says.

"With what?"

He shakes his head. "With everything. With Allison. With my dreams. With . . ."

Tommy starts to say his faith but doesn't. He can't. He won't.

Yet he still feels something inside. This restlessness, these voices, this nudging.

No, I'm tired and it's just . . . It's everything.

He ignores the feelings inside.

"You think we're safe here?" Sam asks.

"I hope. Yeah, I think it's over. I think we'll be okay."

He looks outside the opening of the tent. In the background is a massive fire pit. Tommy sees that men are throwing dead bodies into the flames.

As he sips his bottled water, Tommy thinks about the last twenty-four hours and specifically about everything that's happened since this morning.

Skylar finding a Bible in the library and then being attacked on the street.

Pastor Shay finally praying a real prayer and giving a real sermon and becoming the real pastor he'd always meant to be. And then being killed in the church hallway.

Dan crying out to God. First in anger, then in fear and sadness and acceptance.

And finally Allison. Knowing and realizing and choosing in her last few moments.

All of them snatched and gutted and thrown away by the evil things out there.

Tommy suddenly has an amazing, awful realization that sends goose bumps all over his body and makes him seize up with fear. "They're drawn to faith," he says out loud.

"What?" Sam asks.

He looks at her, shaking his head, dumbfounded. "They're drawn to faith."

Of course.

Like a light in the darkness attracting moths, faith is the

thing they're drawn to. Like blood to vampires. Like drugs to addicts. Like innocent souls to monsters.

Tommy looks around the tent again but can't find Jack.

Oh no.

He can hear the light echo of fluttering again. He wonders if he's imagining it but he doesn't think so. "We need to find Jack."

Can it be that simple? That easy? That one simple act and decision can lead to your demise?

He grabs Sam's arm as he leads her out of the tent looking for their last remaining friend.

They find another tent, this one with a line of people all waiting to step up to a large, circular tub full of water and then . . .

Be baptized.

The chaplain Jack was talking to is up there and . . .

No no no please no.

It can't happen this way, this quickly, this suddenly.

The fluttering sounds are getting louder now.

Just like always.

Not again please God no.

Then he sees a figure coming up out of the water, holding his breath, opening his eyes, smiling.

Jack is smiling.

It's been some time since Tommy's seen that smile.

"Jack!"

Tommy can't believe this. It's crazy. They weave through the crowd as they hear the words of the chaplain.

"Baptism is an outward sign of an inward commitment. It is also like taking the witness stand to declare the truth of the gospel to all who are present."

The thumping and the high-pitched wailing are followed by sudden screams. Howls of horror from spectators and strangers around them.

Suddenly the chaplain is swatted like a bug and sent flying into the back of the tent. They still can't see what did it but they can hear those nasty sounds, loud and horrific like massive bugs scampering all around them.

Jack is picked up.

Tommy tries to get to him but the crowd suddenly goes wild and disperses, knocking him down.

When Tommy looks up, Jack is hovering horizontal, several feet off the ground, the water dripping from him, his arms hanging down.

Tommy shouts Jack's name again but his voice seems to be lost in the chaos. Jack is struggling to get free but can't move. Something has him. Something is holding him up.

Then Jack's body folds up like a flip phone. His legs snap right over his chest. There's a violent, sickly cracking sound and a howling. Jack's body is shaken for a moment, then thrown into the air over Tommy and everyone.

The whipping sounds cut into the air all around them like machine-gun fire ripping through the night. Tommy knows Jack is dead and knows he and Sam have to get out of here. He grabs her hand and they run.

His head is a gushing waterfall, his gut and soul falling

fragments. Everything races and rushes and nothing feels good.

They run. And they keep running.

The snapping sounds of Jack's crushing bones and back run with him.

The relief center has now turned into a death zone. Everybody is running with nowhere to run to. Fires are breaking out. The living and the dead have become interchangeable. Any respite is now gone.

Tommy doesn't let go of Sam's hand even as she slips and falls. He keeps moving and drags her along. Scared, stampeding people smother them, yet they keep moving.

There's still a way. There's still hope.

Yet he knows every single soul around them realizes they're all doomed.

They're all going to die.

53
THE RIGHT MOMENT

They're running back toward the bridge when Sam suddenly stops and pulls Tommy to her.

"Come on," he screams at her.

He lets go of her hand for a moment as she stands there while a sea of people flow all around them. For some insane reason she's stopping.

"I can't," Sam says. "Not anymore."

Tommy shakes his head. "What are you doing?"

"There's only one way, Tommy. We have to make a choice. You know it. Allison did too. Even Jack did."

Tommy just wants to run. He wants to run and turn his back on all this and keep running.

Like I've done my whole life.

"They made the right choice," Sam says.

Tommy blinks and knows she's just being honest. He doesn't have to see anything more to realize it's the truth.

Sam looks at Tommy while she tries to hold back tears. "The choice is ours, Tommy. It has been all along."

She offers him a hand.

"There are other believers out there," she says. "I'm gonna find them. We can find them. Before it's too late."

Tommy doesn't take her hand, however.

He's still resisting.

Still wanting to do it his way.

Still wanting to control things.

Sam gives him a mournful glance. She begins walking away.

"Don't go," he calls out. "We're safer here. They're attracted to faith."

Her body starts to get lost in the crowd.

"Choose God, Tommy. Choose Christ. I choose. I believe. I ask for forgiveness for not believing when I should have."

The thudding sound of wings surrounds them. There's wailing and more screaming. The people around him cry out but Tommy can no longer see Sam.

He looks up to the skies.

They've begun to glow, turning bloodred. The clouds are parting like two thunderous doors opening.

Then comes the piercing, blaring noise.

It's another trumpet. Another announcement of doom.

The skies continue to bleed out. Figures—horrible, haunting things—start to fill the sky. Hundreds, maybe thousands of them.

Spilling out.

Coming down.

Rushing down to them.

This is the end.

Tommy is alone now.

He stares at all these people running and cowering around him. All faceless, nameless, meaningless. All those who meant something to him are gone. Even the young, starry-eyed girl who followed him has disappeared.

Everybody is gone.

Why, God?

Why?

Why are You hounding me?

Why do You keep chasing after me?

Dizzy, Tommy wants to just fall down. To sleep. To go away. To make it all go away.

The noise around him begins to fade. The commotion and chaos begin to close down.

But the questions inside continue.

Did You create all of this only to break it?

Did You make something only to mess it all back up?

But the answers come right after the questions.

The answers resound inside. In his mind and his heart.

He hears Allison's words.

"We either choose to accept and believe and get life or we end up dying anyway."

Tommy knows God didn't cause this evil in the world. It was everybody else who did that.

It's me.

He couldn't have cared less for God his whole life, and he still wonders. He still doesn't know. Isn't sure. Doesn't quite understand.

After all this carnage and chaos, Tommy still has doubts.

Doubting Thomas. That's who I am.

But his heart and soul long for something. For some kind of meaning. For something deeper. For the kind of deep love and grace that his friends all found before the end.

He's afraid of the skies, the ground, the way his heart pounds. Of this pitch-black night and the hovering shadows inside it. His knees fall to the dirt beneath him. His hands feel good clenched as tight as they can be. His eyes are wide open without blinking.

Are You really up there watching? Do You really care?

This tiny place. Is this where it all ends? Or . . .

Is it where it finally begins?

Tommy hears it calling after him. The peace, the love, the hope.

There's still time. There's still a chance. You can still choose.

From somewhere, a surge of something begins to fill him.

He's been running for so long. Trying. Ignoring. Burning. Wondering.

God, is there a place up there for me?

A breath exhaled. Heavy, hurting.

God would You really love me? Have You always loved me?

Tommy no longer feels foolish for praying these prayers. The world has ended and there's no time and no need to feel ashamed anymore. Pride has been tossed out the broken back window. He still doesn't know. He's still not so sure that he can do this. That God will really love him and accept him and . . .

Save me.

But he swallows and feels his dry mouth and he decides to speak his words out loud.

"God, please save me. I'm sorry. For ignoring You. For not listening. For not caring. Please save me. I need You. I can't—there's nothing else. Nothing left. I have nothing. I need You."

Tommy shivers. Closes his eyes and wipes the tears away.

There are more screams now. More running feet and ransacking tents and fires raging all around.

But for Tommy, there's silence in his soul. A peaceful sort of quiet.

"I need You now."

His bones ache. He feels something. But more than that, it's what he *doesn't* feel. Something leaves. Something—a whole lot of somethings—suddenly leave those legs and shoulders and muscles and bones. The weary world decides to finally depart. The weight clawing at his conscience finally dissolves.

He feels . . .

Free.

For a moment. For just a moment. But it's okay.

It's okay.

He knows God does love and does accept him. Yes. Sure. Of course it's crazy and he doesn't understand other than knowing that he feels lighter. He feels like someone who can finally stand up. Stand strong.

Stand right.

So he does.

Tommy breathes out a sigh of relief and stands up and sees the nightmare unfolding all around him. But the eyes he looks through are different now.

Sometimes it has seemed like his whole life revolved around watching and waiting. Watching for the right moment, waiting for the right memory to capture.

Hoping for that perfect minute where everything finally comes together.

But Tommy knows now that moment was always there for the taking. He was just too stubborn and stupid and self-satisfied to ever fully embrace it.

Until now.

The pandemonium around him makes him want to run. But he knows he no longer has to.

They're coming for him. They will soon catch him.

But Tommy's no longer afraid.